THUNDER AND CLUCK

The Brave Friend Leads the Way!

For Bennett & Lawson
—J. E.

With Love for My Old Man,
who gave me the Sea.
Thank you, Dad.
—M. T.

SIMON SPOTLIGHT
An imprint of Simon & Schuster Children's Publishing Division
1230 Avenue of the Americas, New York, New York 10020
This Simon Spotlight edition August 2021
Text copyright © 2021 by Jill Esbaum
Illustrations copyright © 2021 by Christopher M. Thompson
All rights reserved, including the right of reproduction in whole or in part in any form.
SIMON SPOTLIGHT, READY-TO-READ, and colophon are registered trademarks
of Simon & Schuster, Inc. For information about special discounts for bulk
purchases, please contact Simon & Schuster Special Sales at 1-866-506-1949 or
business@simonandschuster.com.
Manufactured in the United States of America 0721 LAK
10 9 8 7 6 5 4 3 2 1
Library of Congress Cataloging-in-Publication Data
Names: Esbaum, Jill, author. | Thompson, Miles (Illustrator), illustrator. | Title: The brave
friend leads the way! / by Jill Esbaum; illustrated by Miles Thompson. | Description: Simon
Spotlight edition. | New York: Simon Spotlight, 2021. | Series: Thunder and Cluck; #2
| Summary: On a hot day, two unlikely dinosaur friends find a dark, cool cave, but who
is brave enough to lead the way in? | Identifiers: LCCN 2021003369 (print) | LCCN
2021003370 (ebook) | ISBN 9781534486553 (hardcover) | ISBN 9781534486546
(paperback) | ISBN 9781534486560 (ebook) | Subjects: LCSH: Graphic novels. | CYAC:
Graphic novels. | Dinosaurs—Fiction. | Courage—Fiction. | Friendship—Fiction. | Humorous
stories. | Classification: LCC PZ7.7.E78 Br 2021 (print) | LCC PZ7.7.E78 (ebook) | DDC
741.5/973—dc23 | LC record available at https://lccn.loc.gov/2021003369 | LC ebook
record available at https://lccn.loc.gov/2021003370

THUNDER AND CLUCK

The Brave Friend Leads the Way!

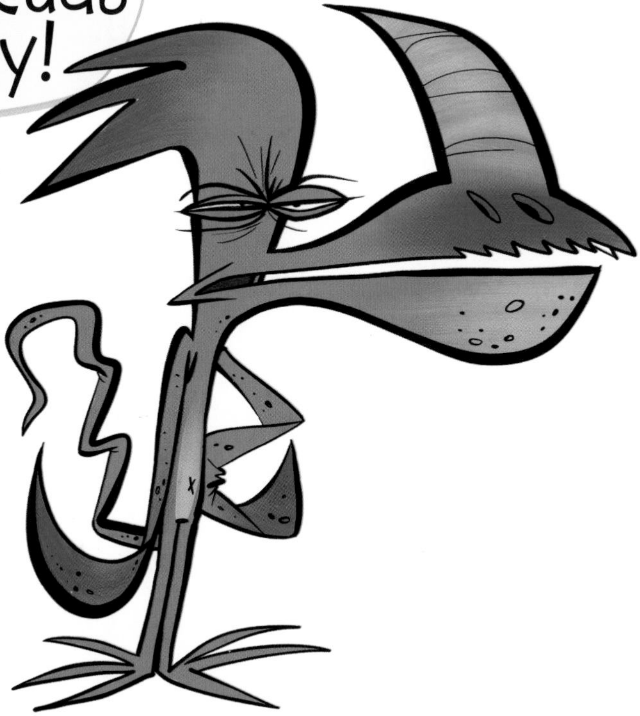

Written by **JILL ESBAUM**
Illustrated by **MILES THOMPSON**

Ready-to-Read *GRAPHICS*

Simon Spotlight
New York London Toronto Sydney New Delhi

HOW TO READ THIS BOOK

THUNDER and CLUCK are here to give you some tips on reading this book.

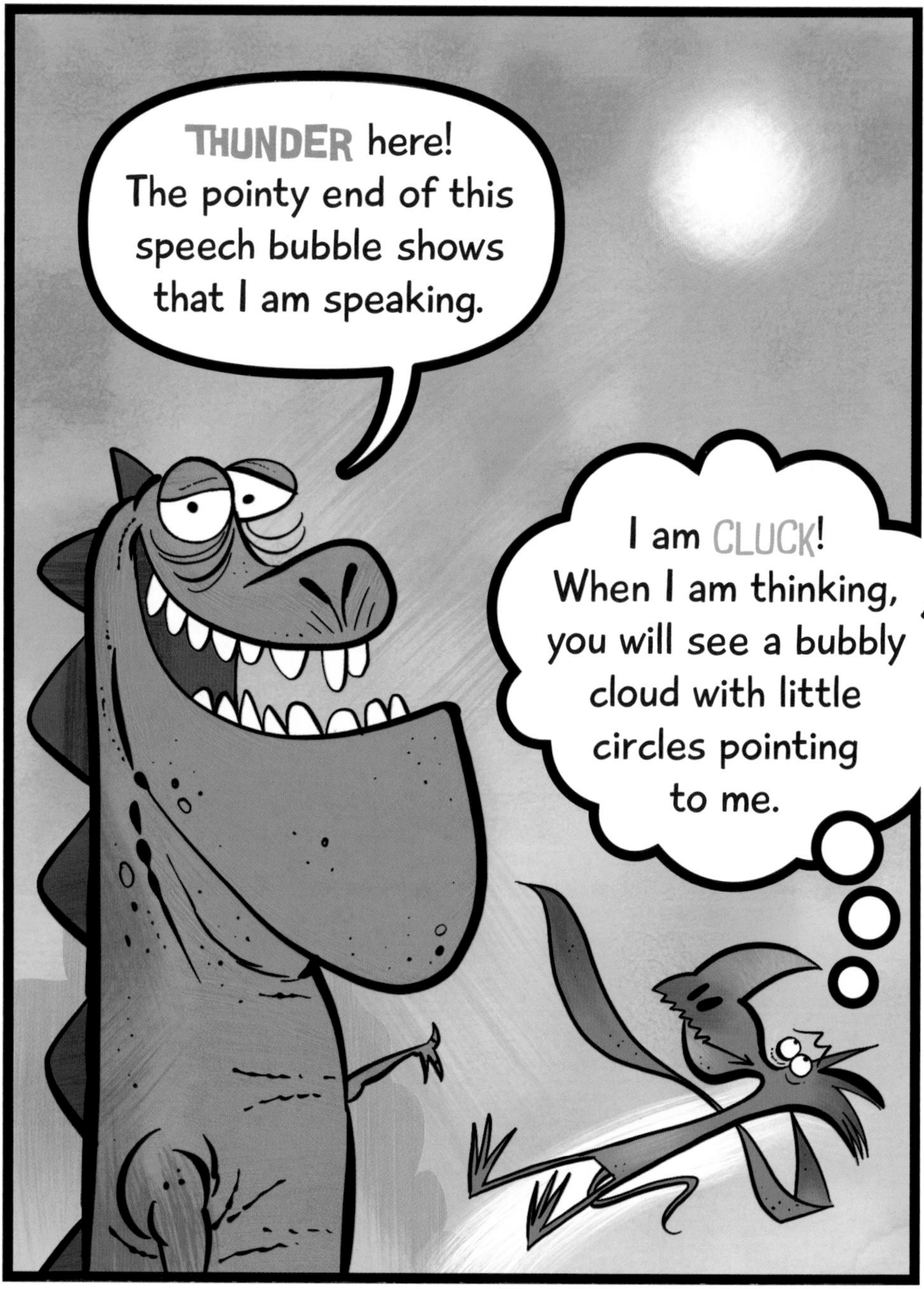
THUNDER here! The pointy end of this speech bubble shows that I am speaking.
I am CLUCK! When I am thinking, you will see a bubbly cloud with little circles pointing to me.

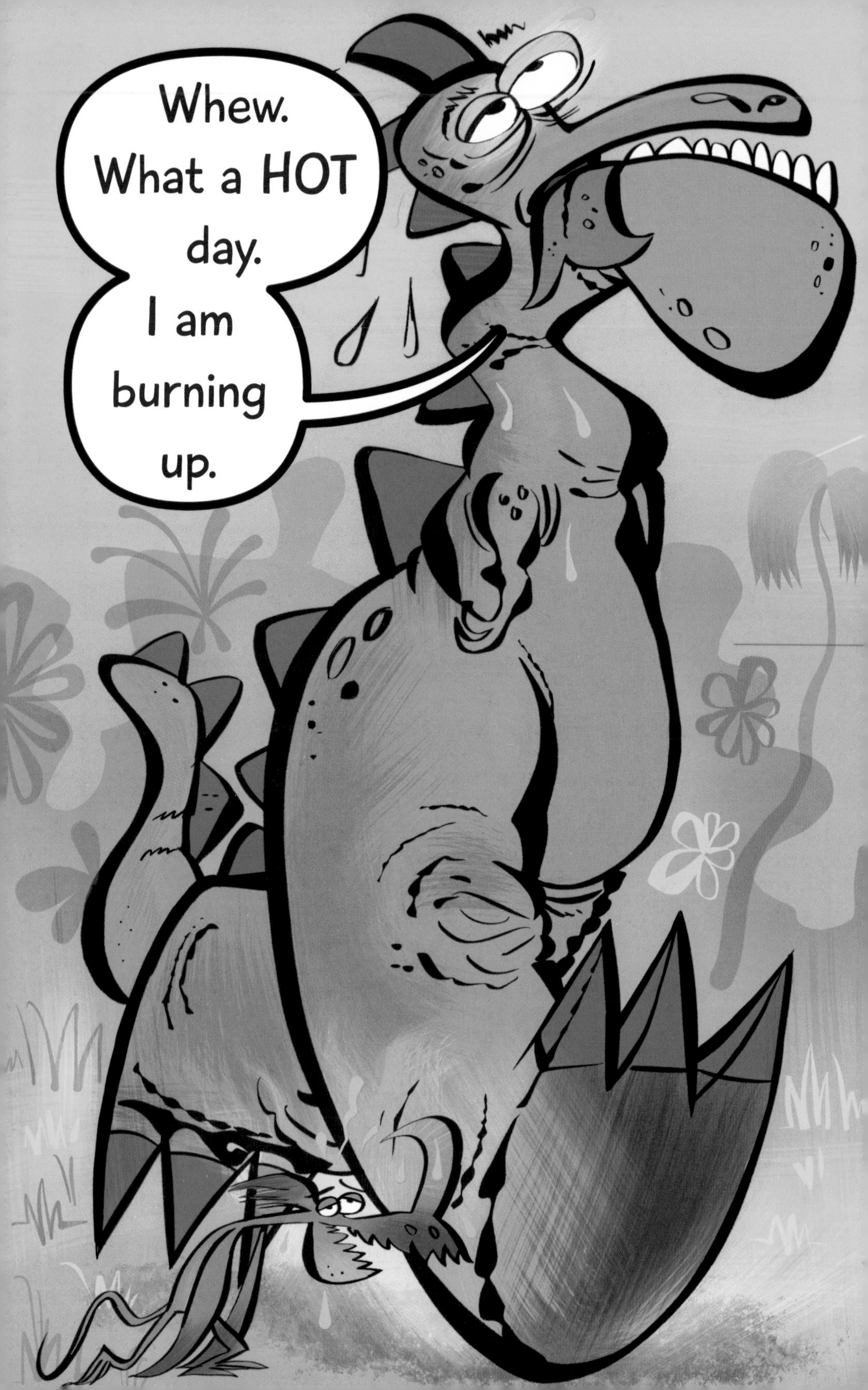
Whew. What a HOT day. I am burning up.

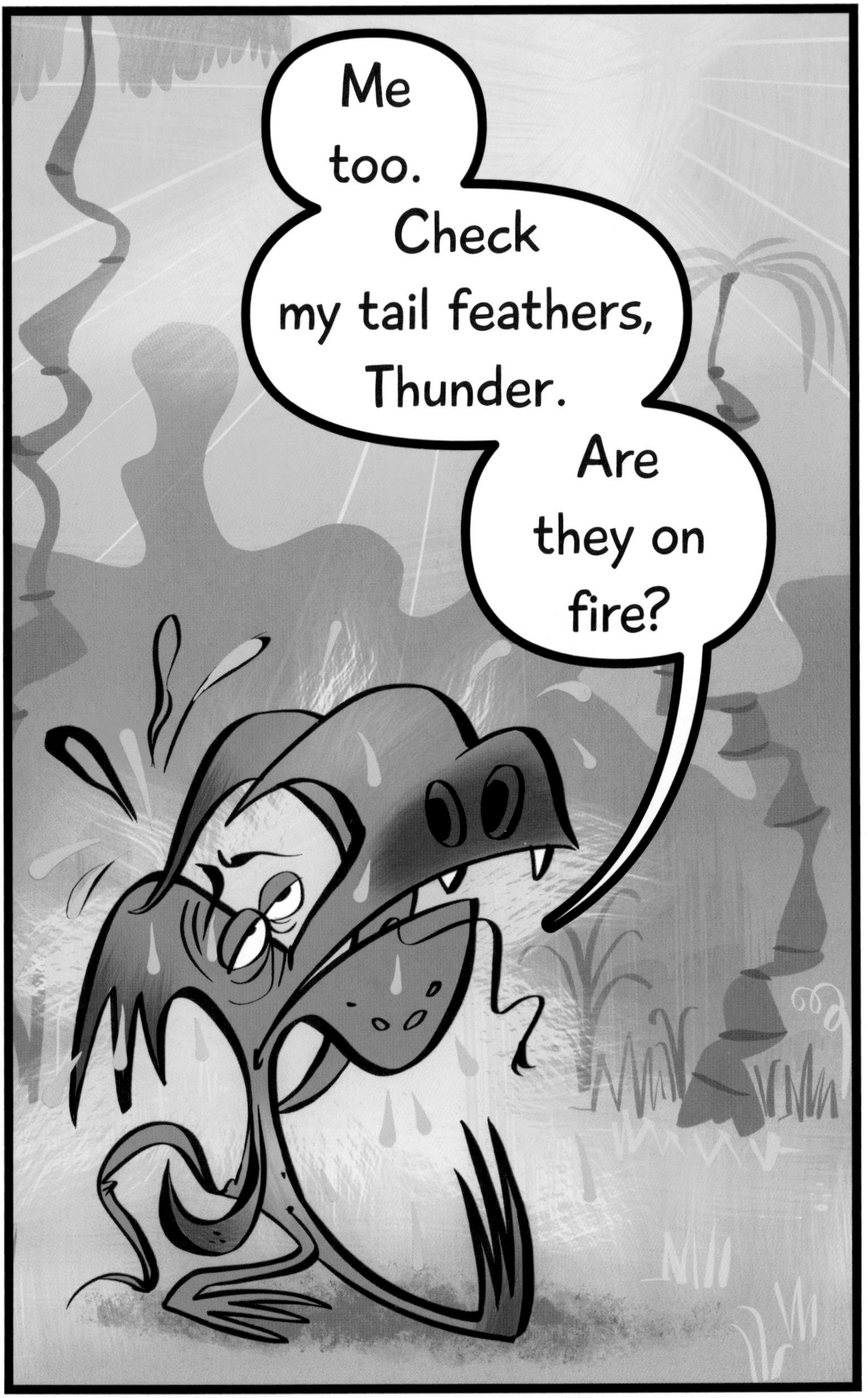
Me too. Check my tail feathers, Thunder. Are they on fire?

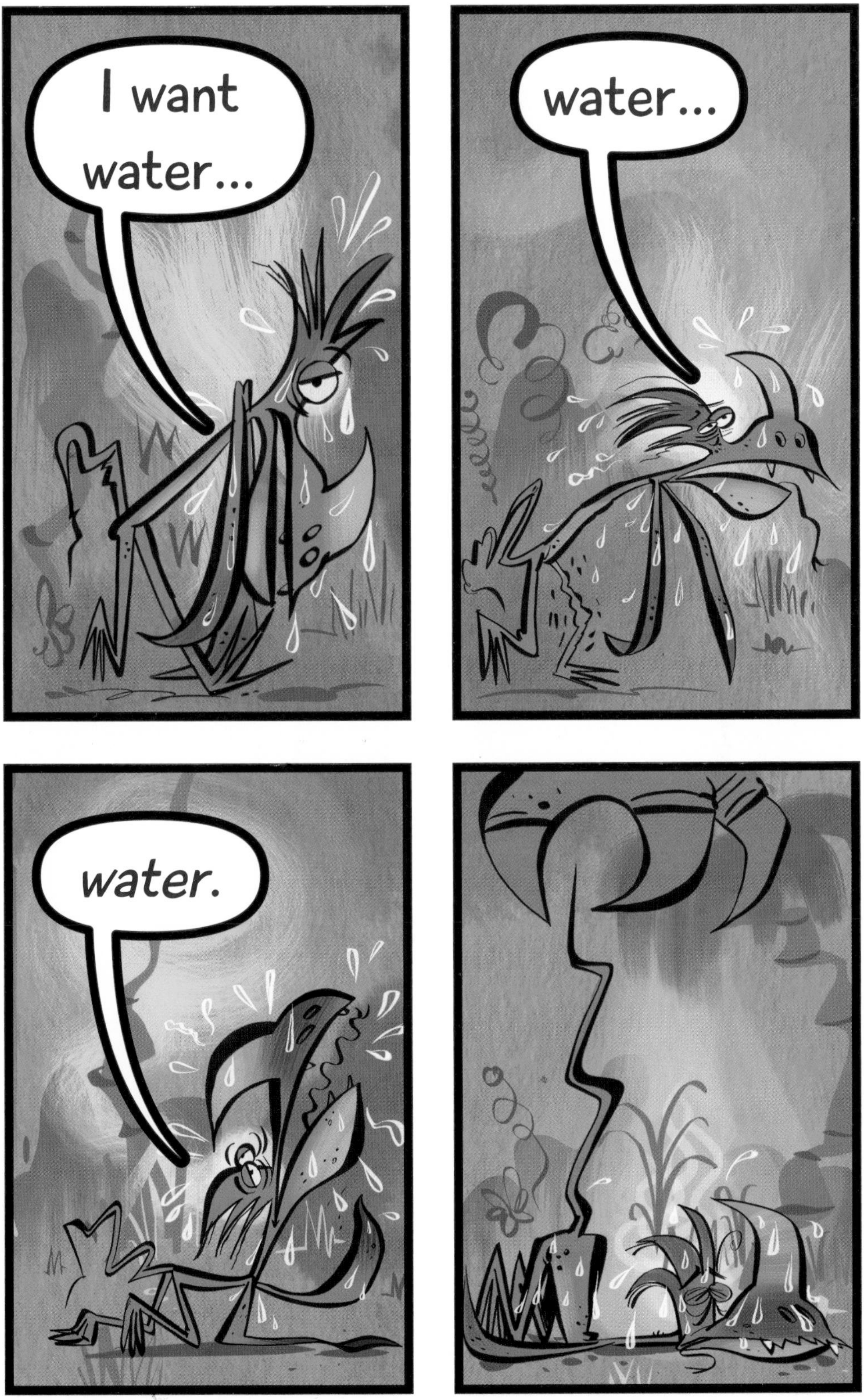
I want water...
water...
water.

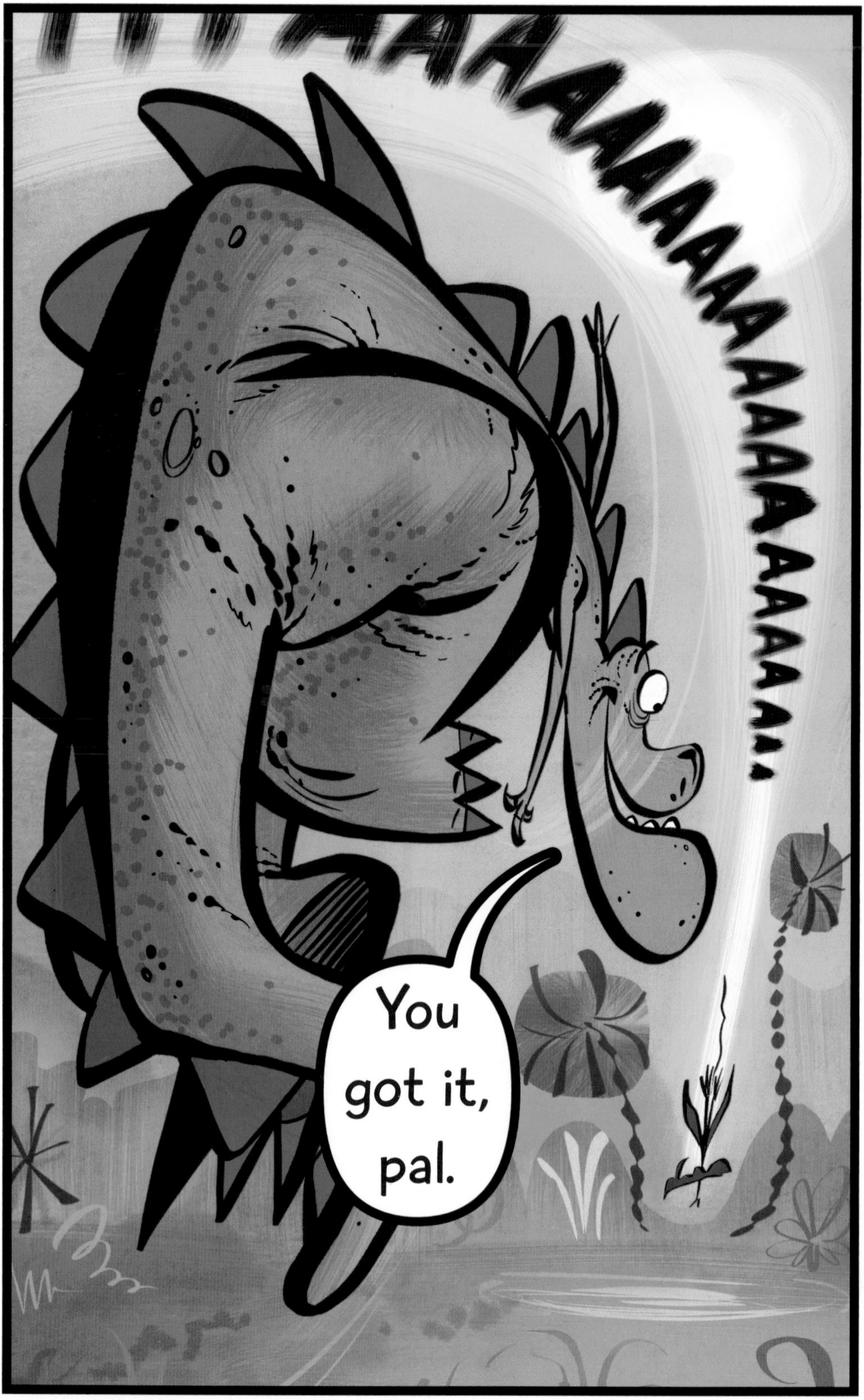
You got it, pal.

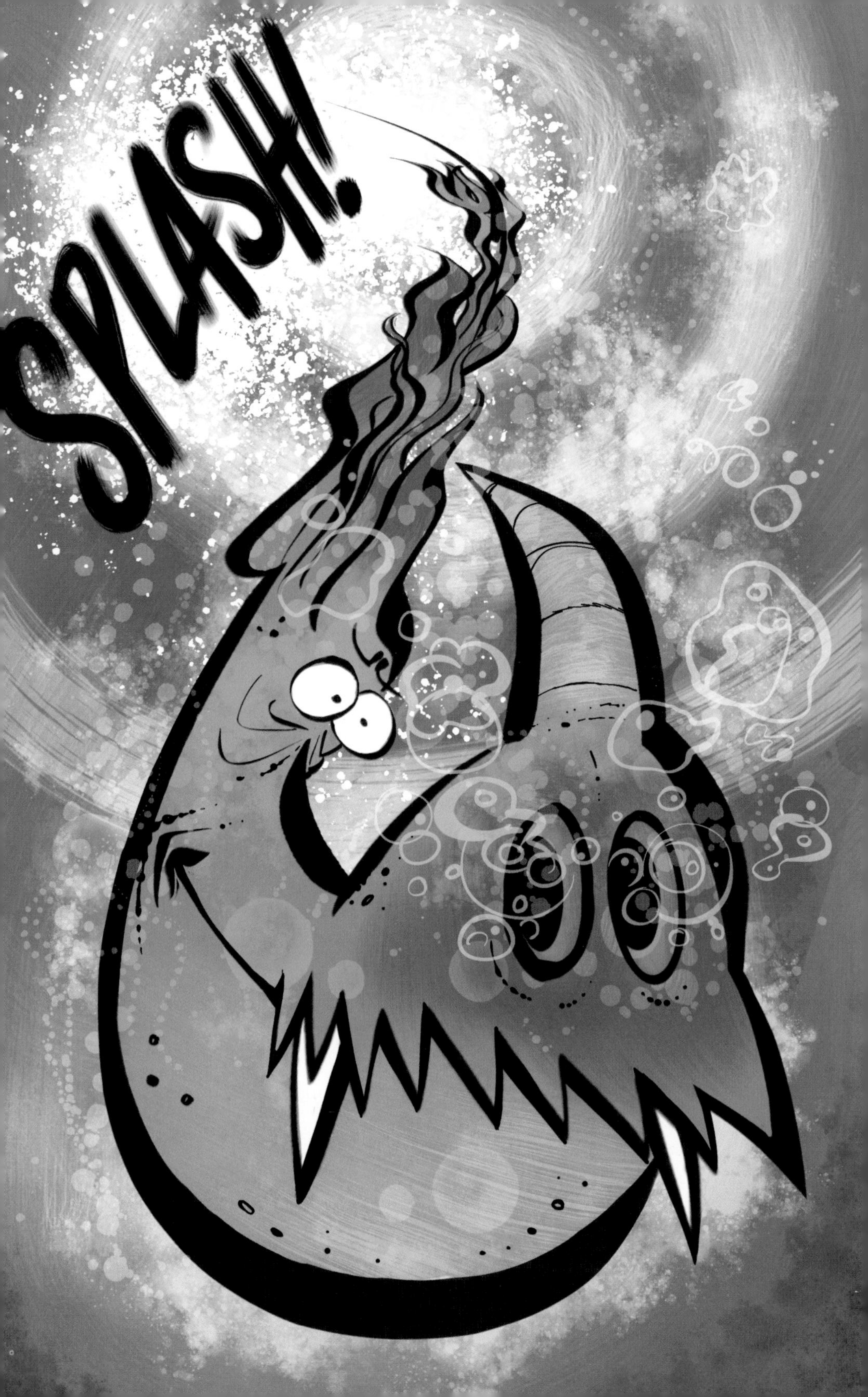
SPLASH!

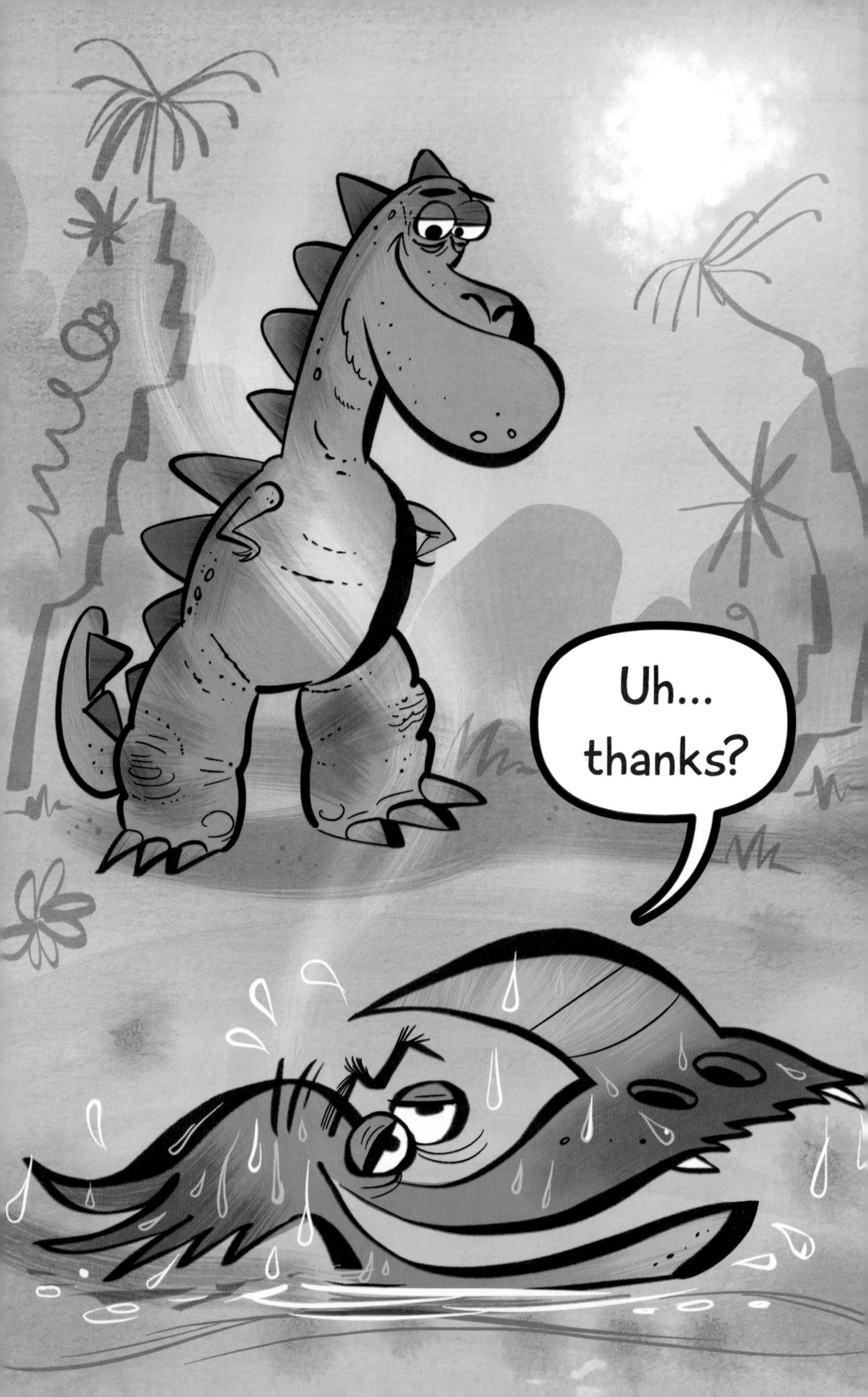
Uh...
thanks?

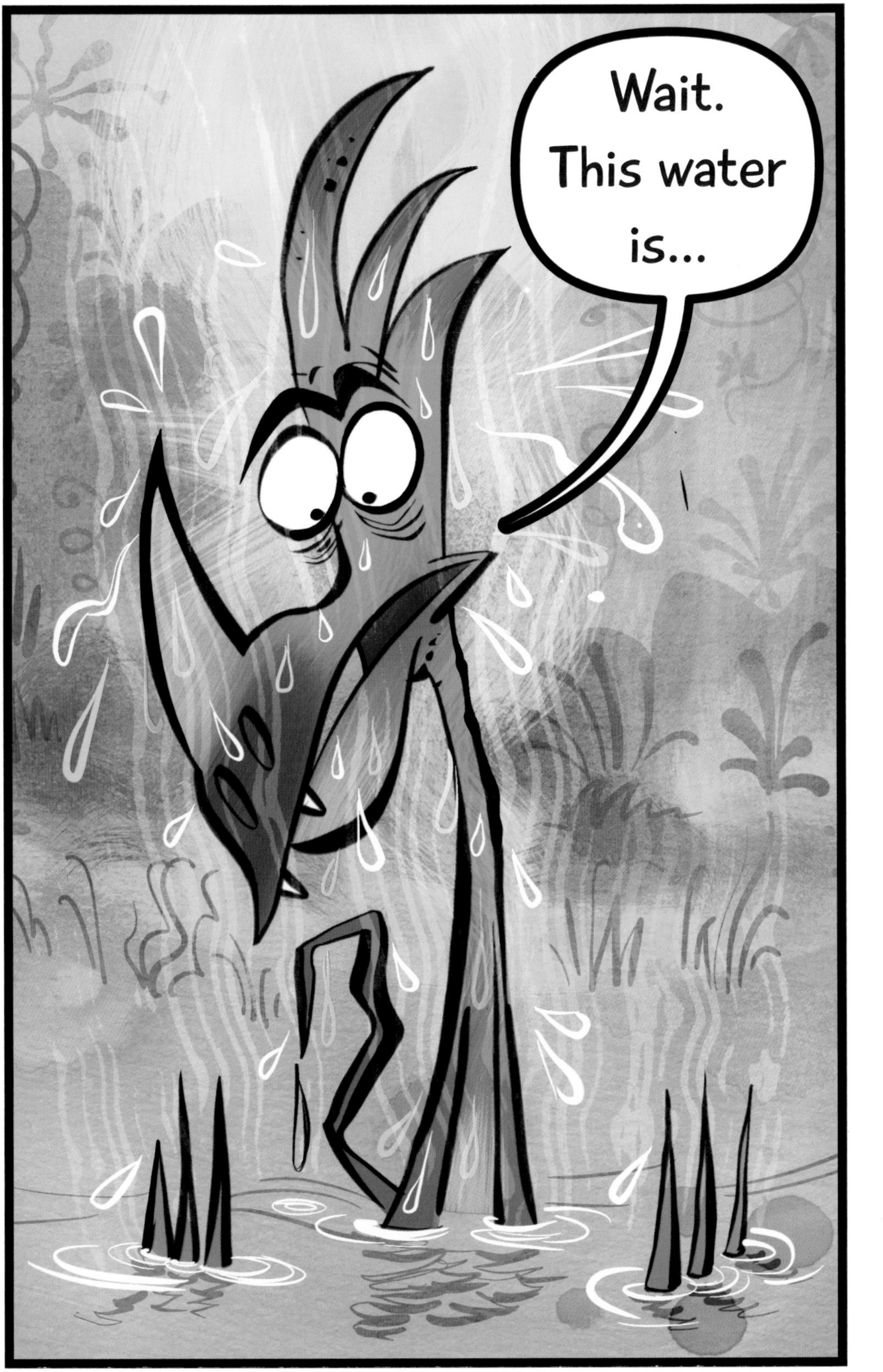
Wait.
This water
is...

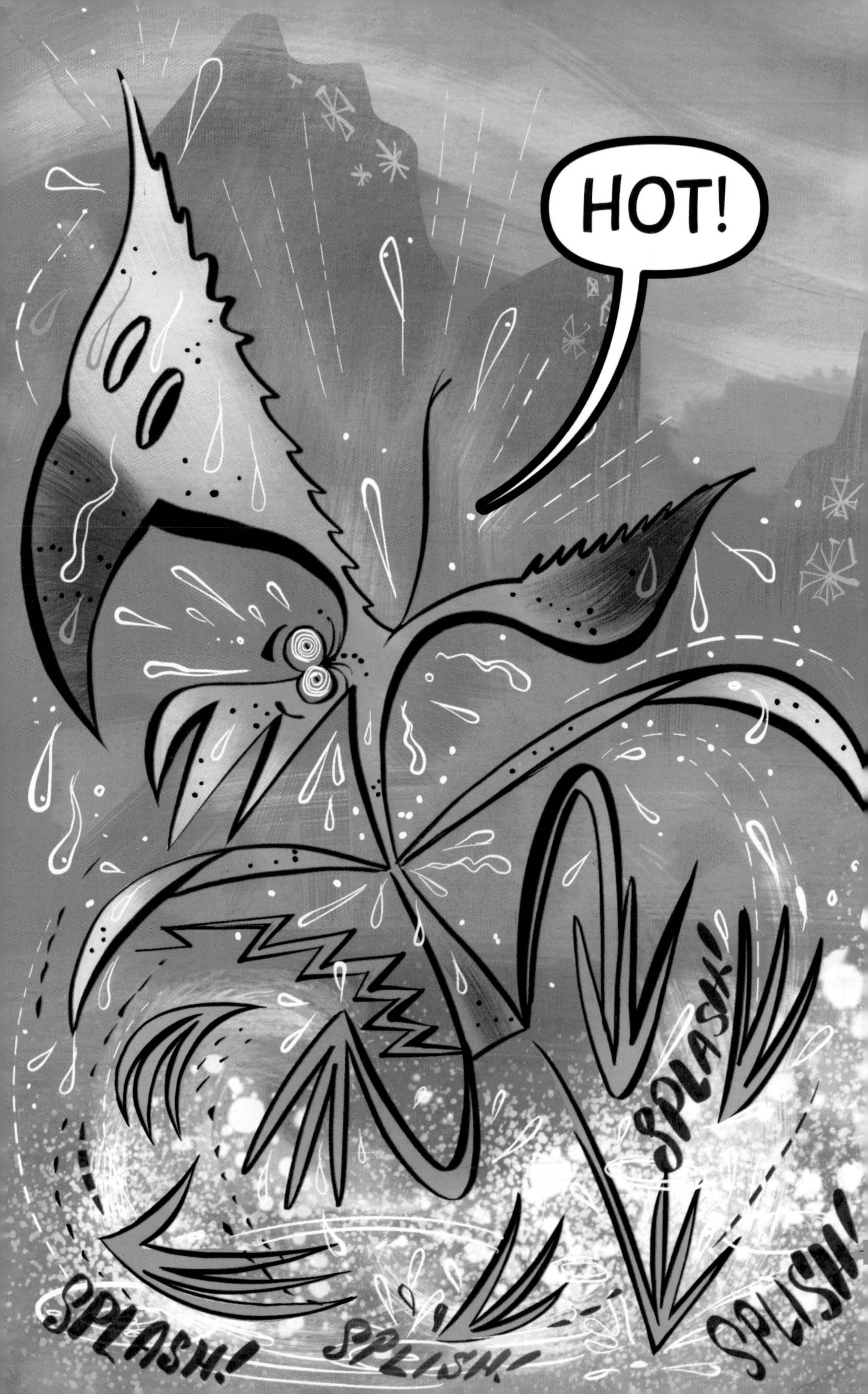
HOT!
SPLASH!
SPLASH!
SPLISH!
SPLISH!

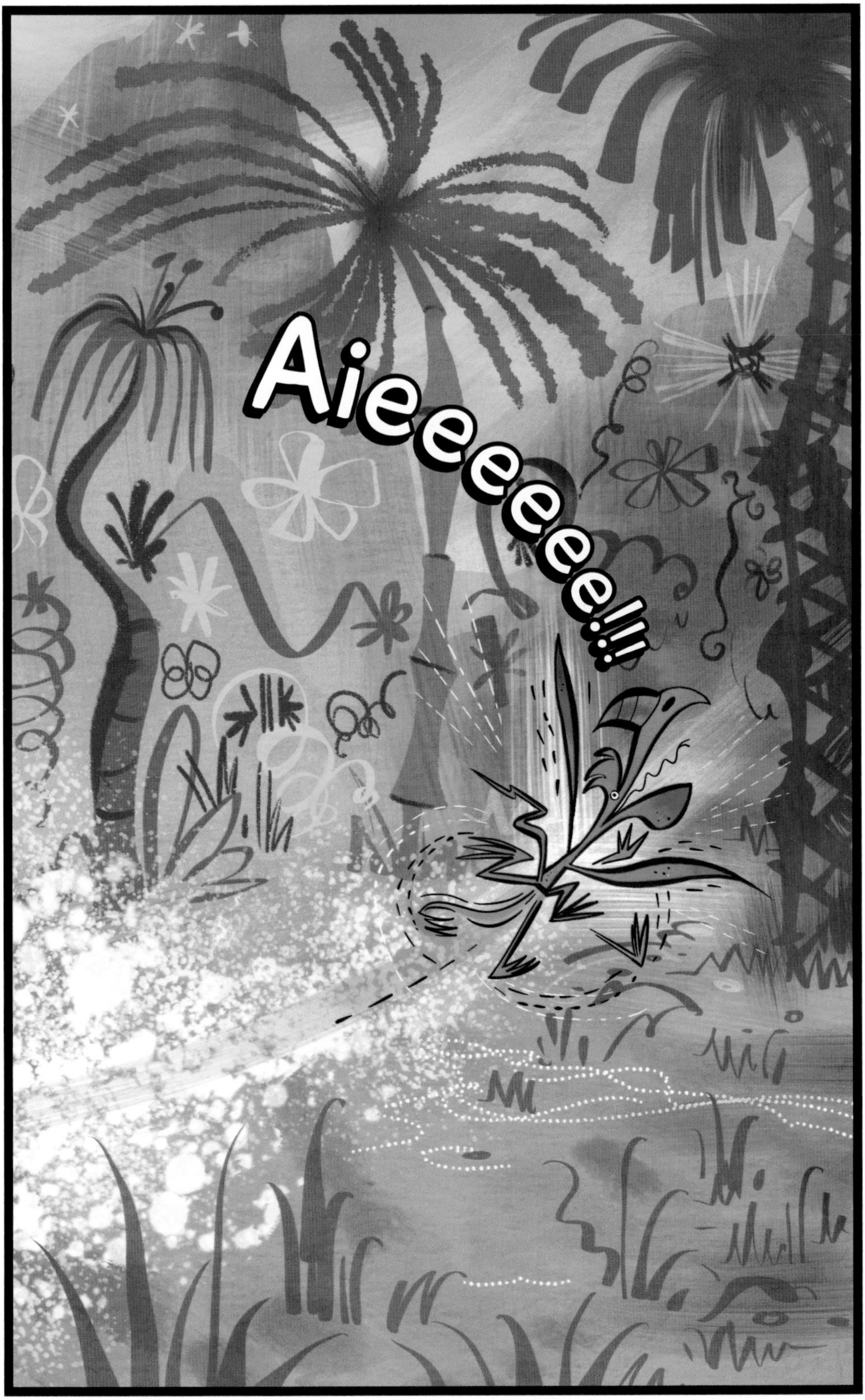
Aieeeeee!!!

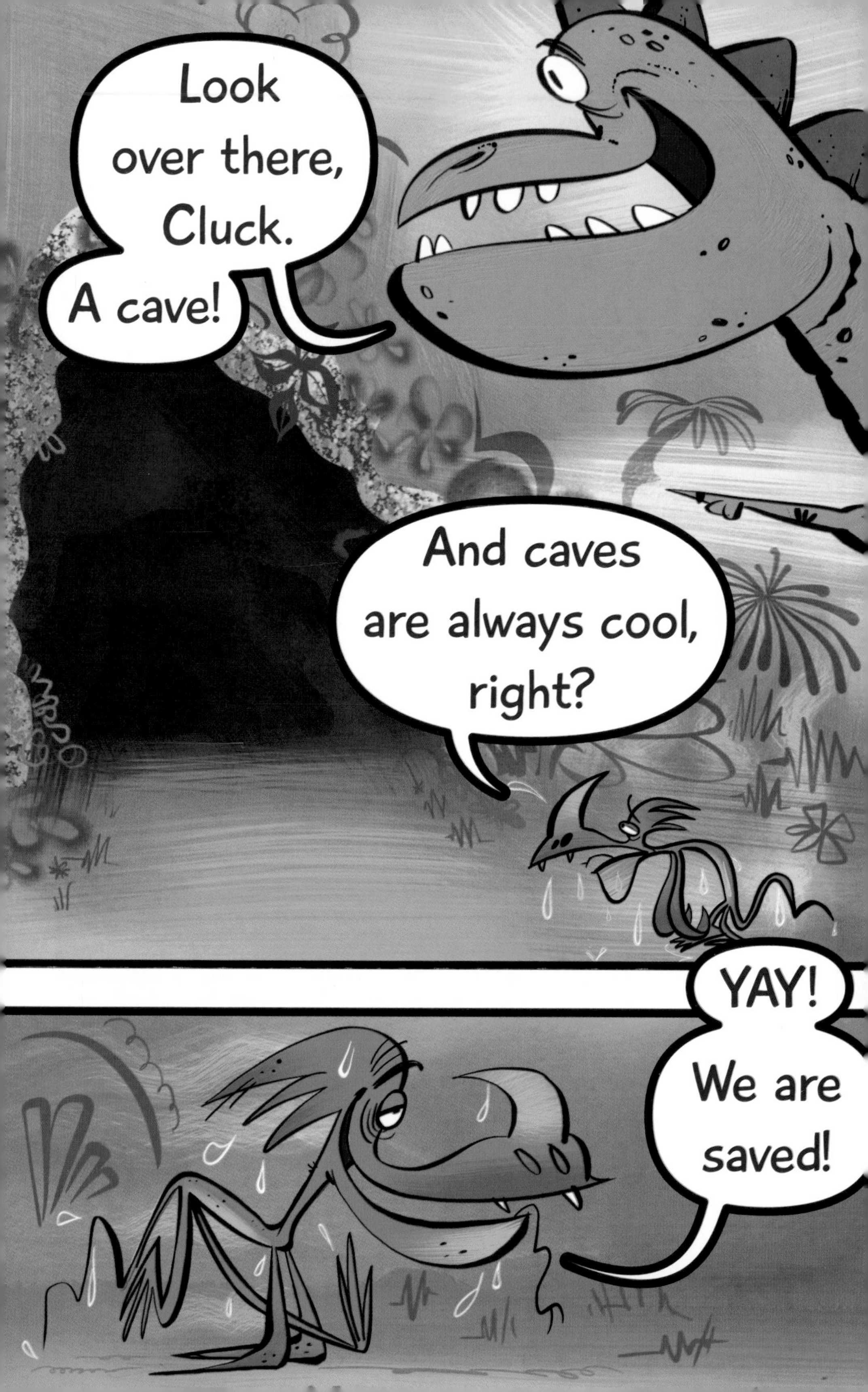
Look over there, Cluck.
A cave!
And caves are always cool, right?
YAY!
We are saved!

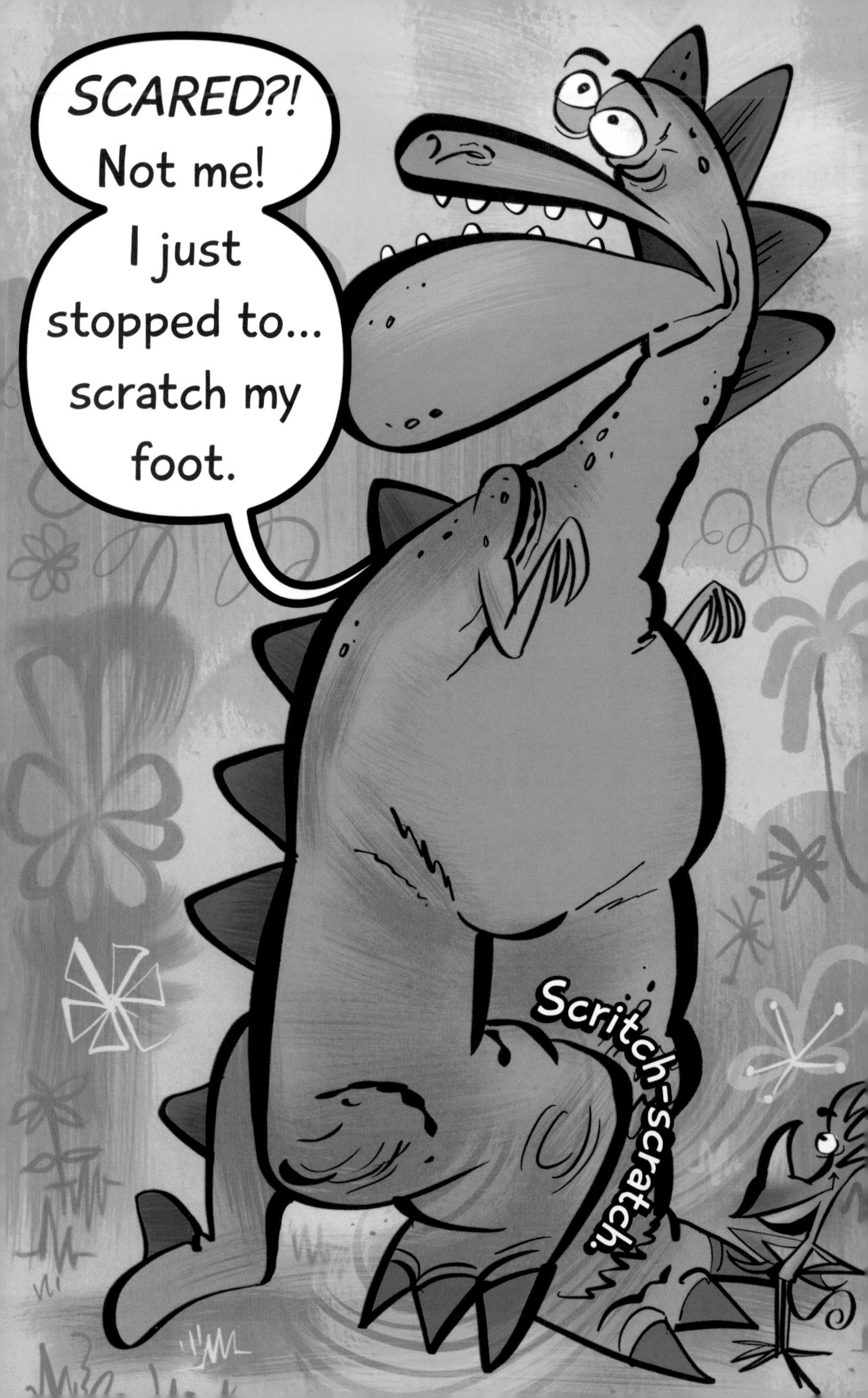
SCARED?! Not me! I just stopped to... scratch my foot.
Scritch-scratch.

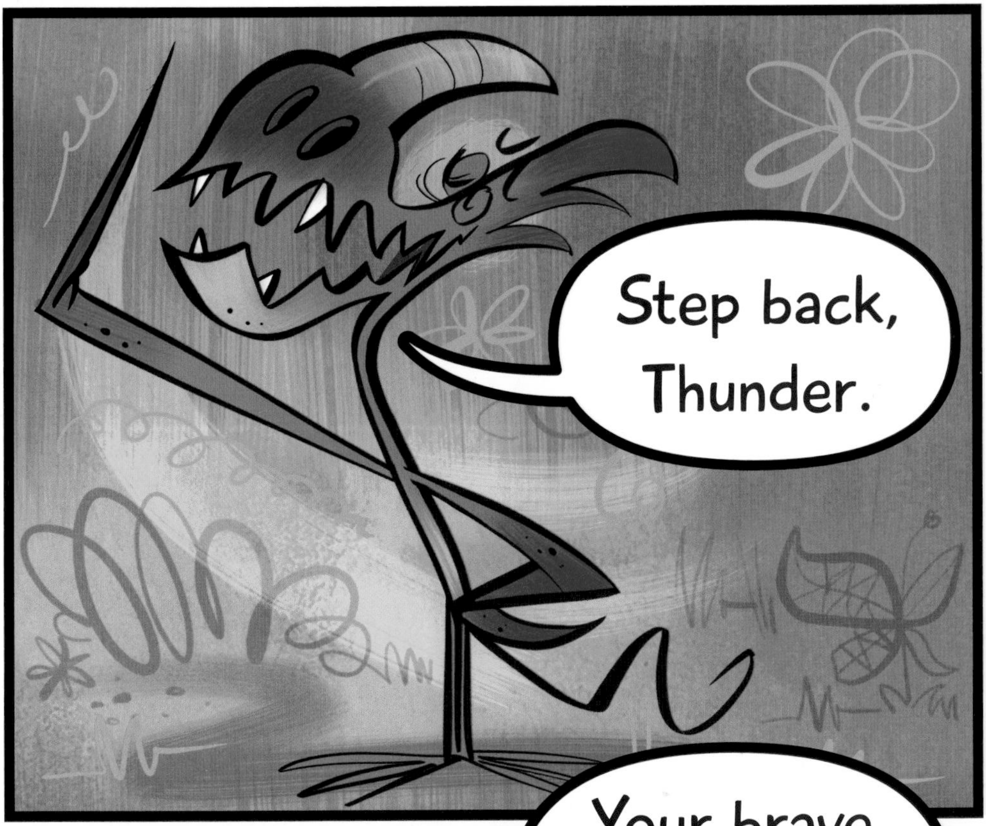
Step back, Thunder.

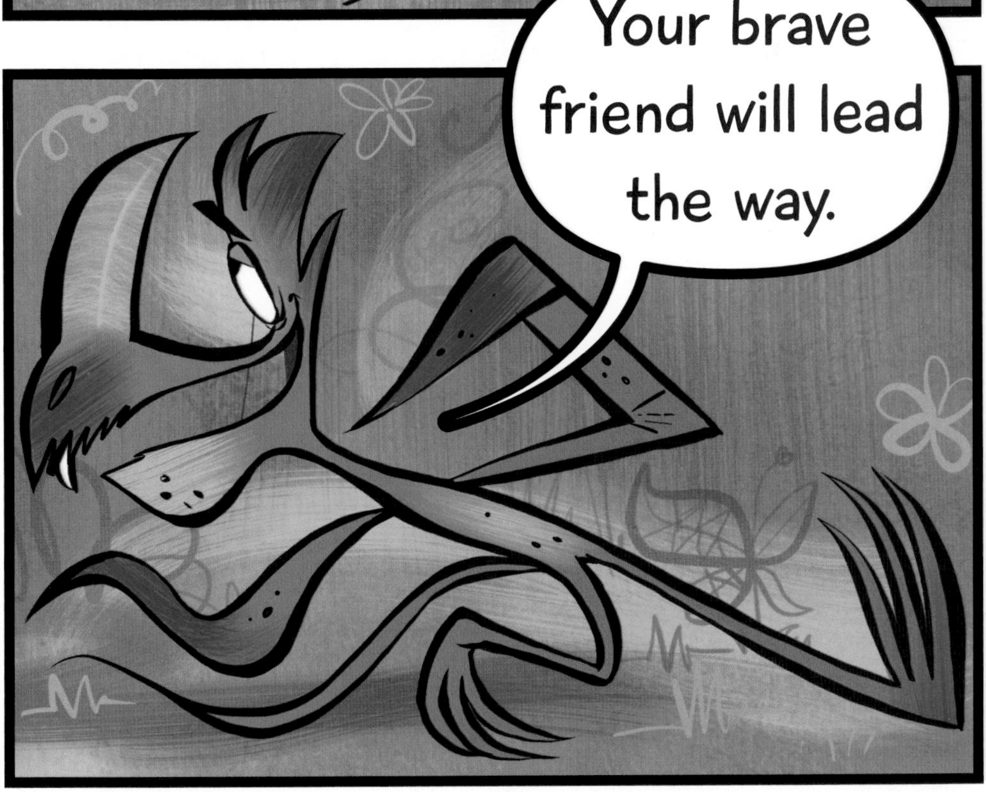
Your brave friend will lead the way.

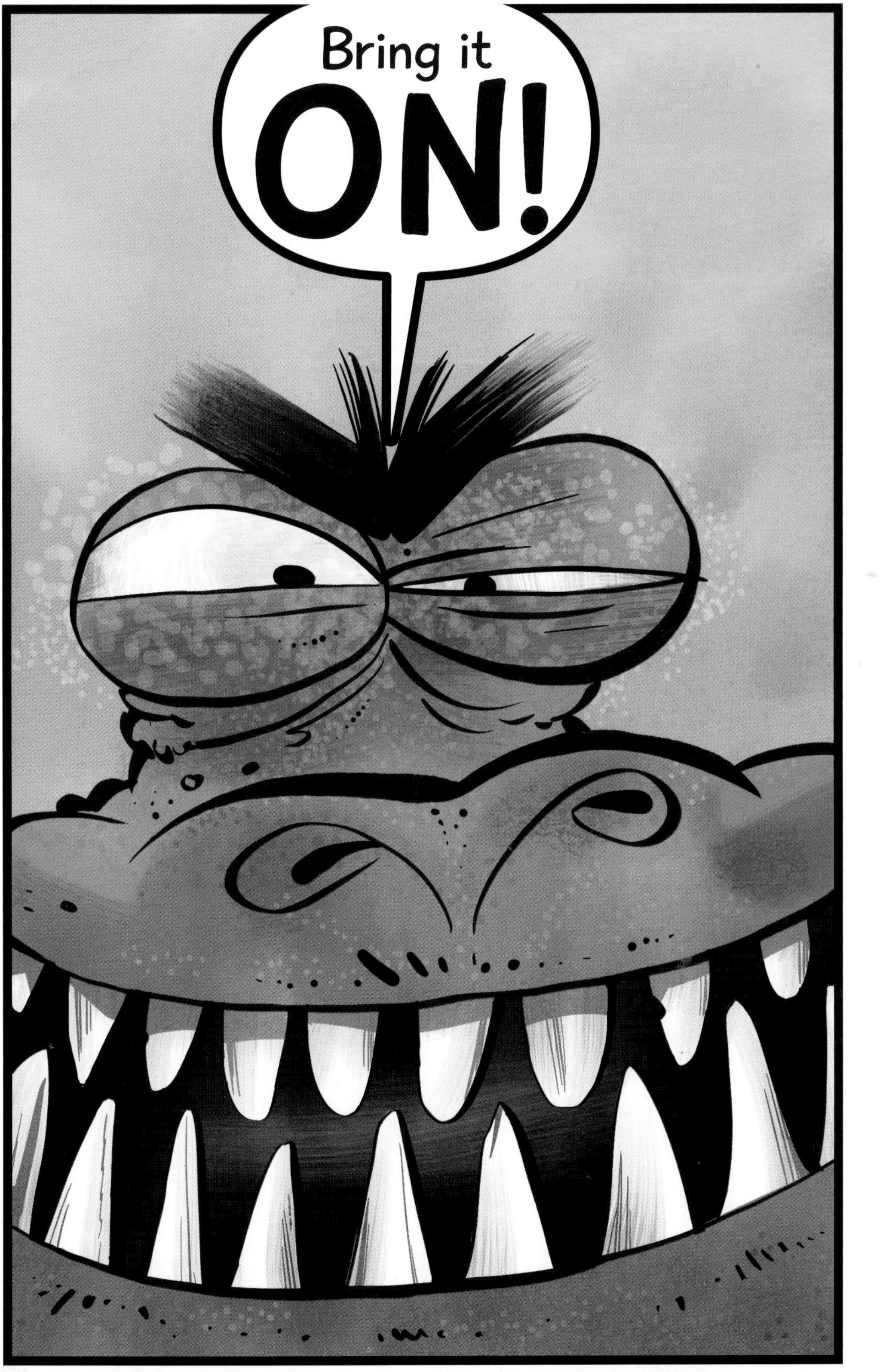
Bring it ON!

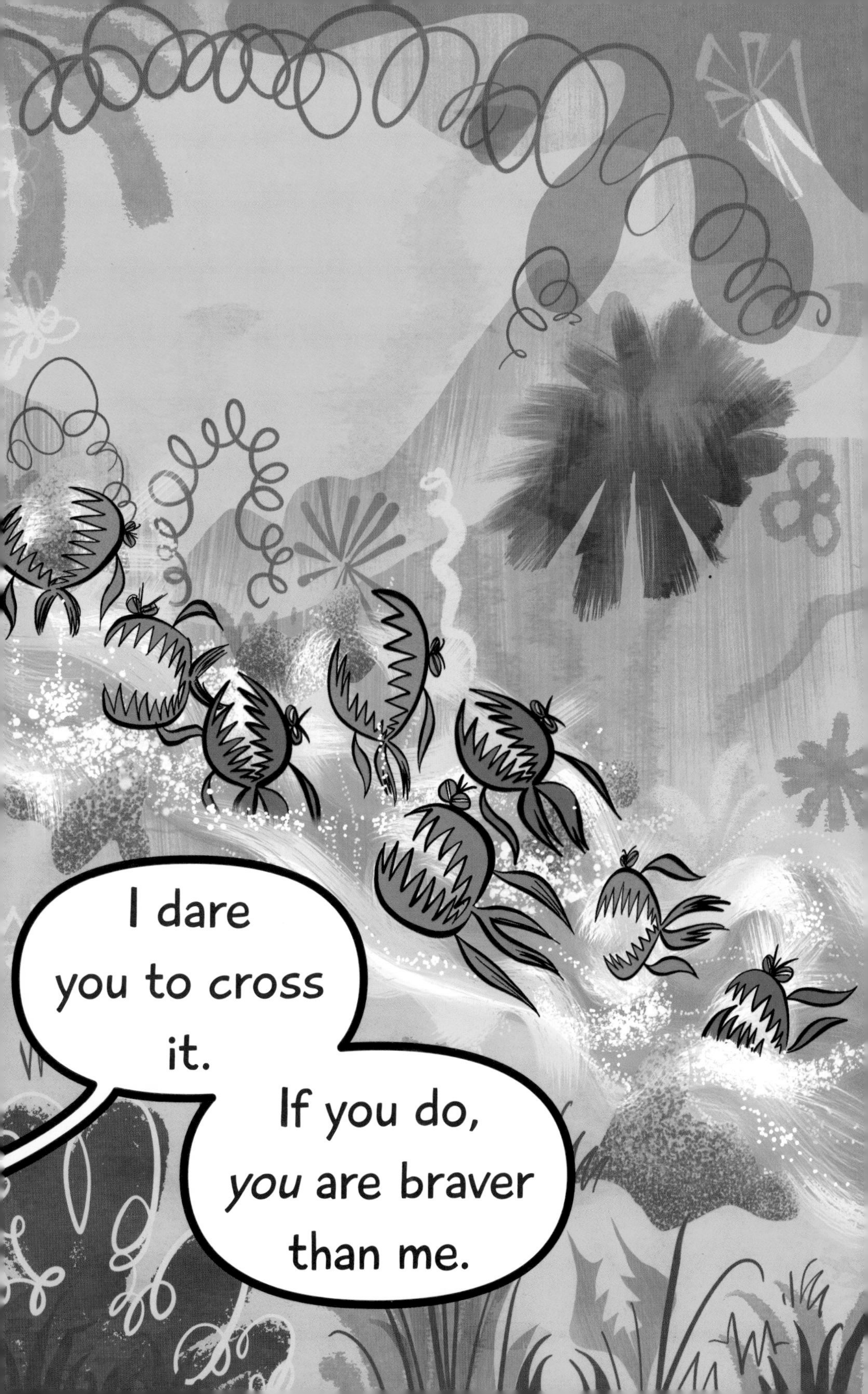
I dare you to cross it.
If you do, *you* are braver than me.

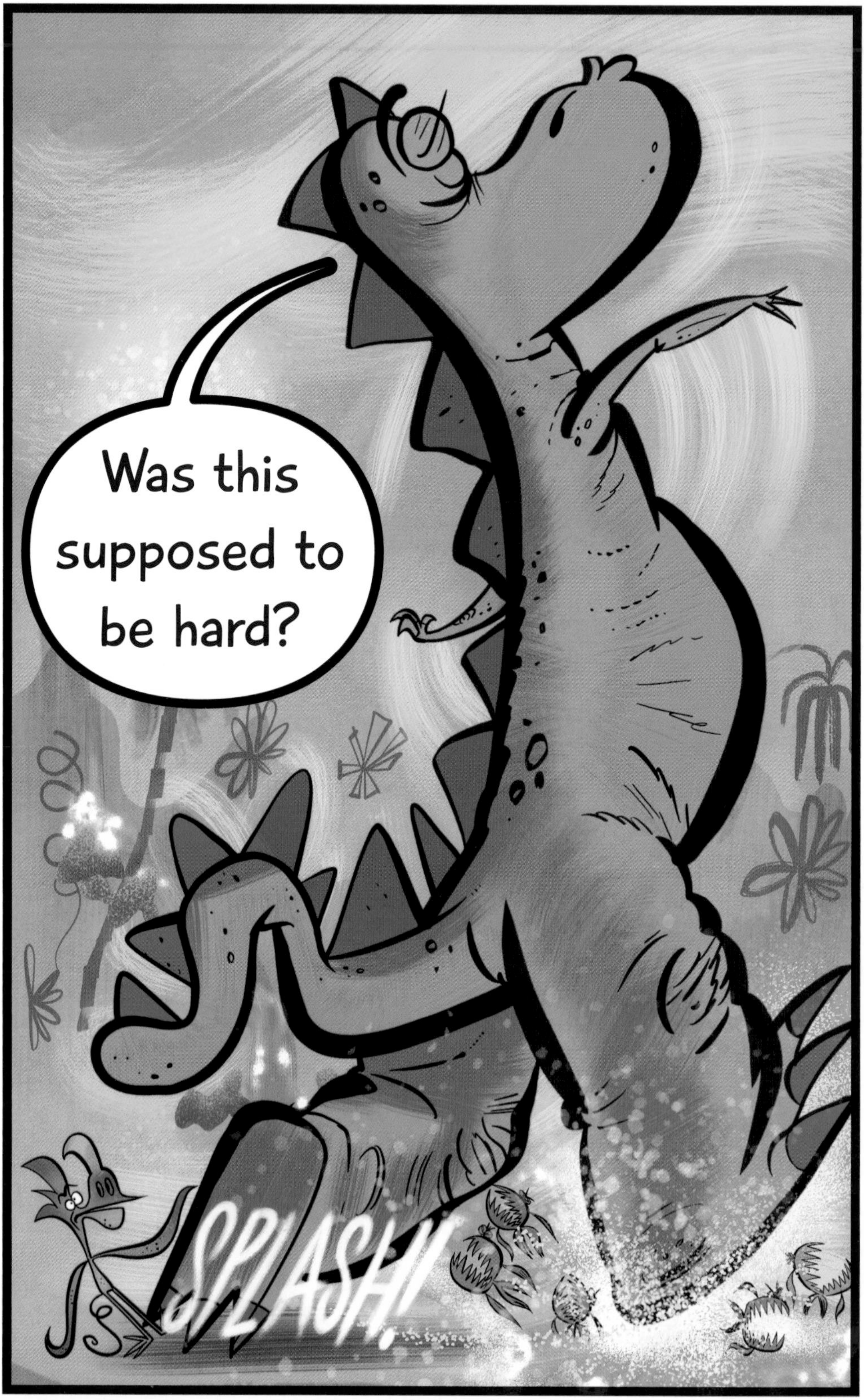
Was this supposed to be hard?
SPLASH!

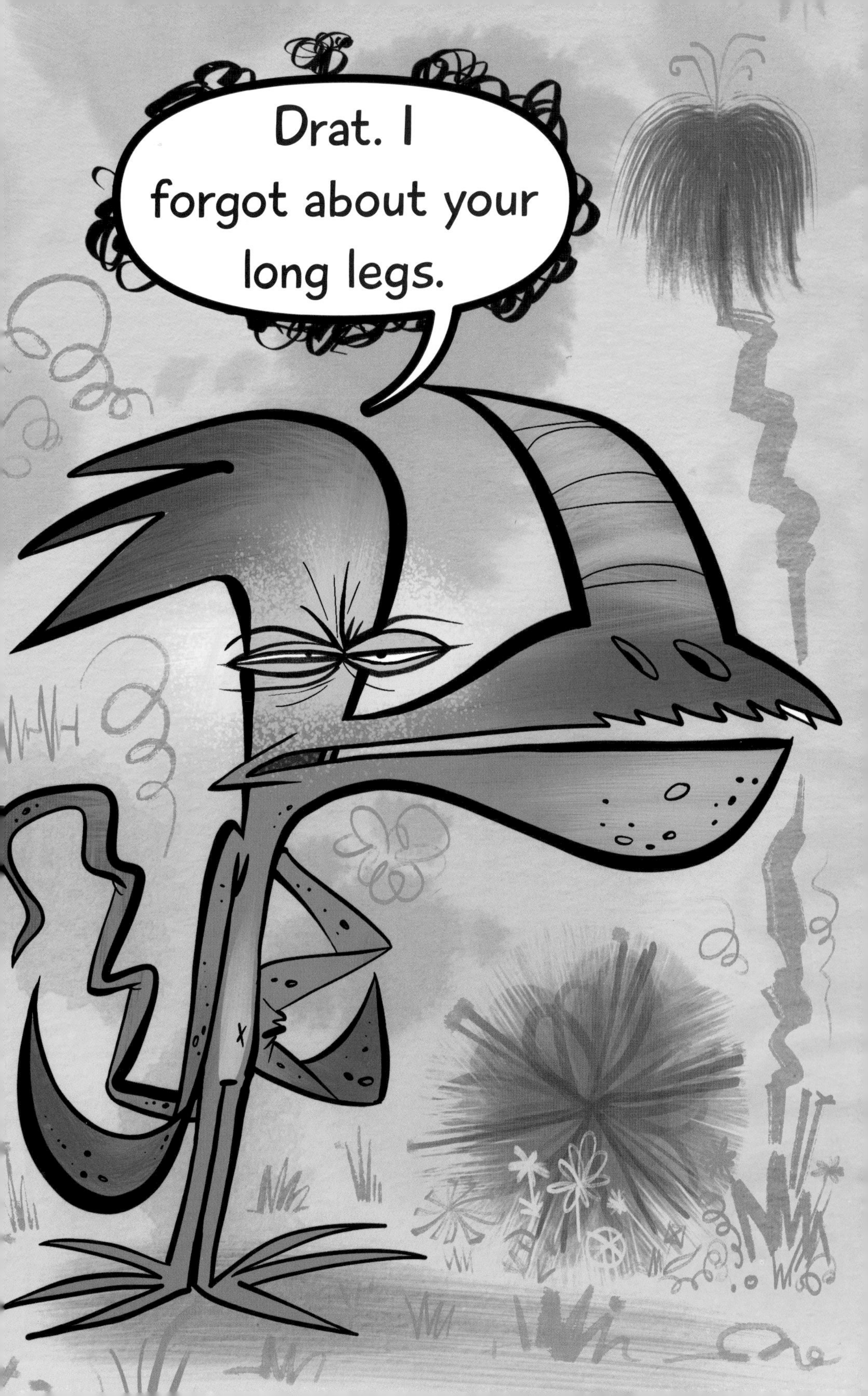
Drat. I forgot about your long legs.

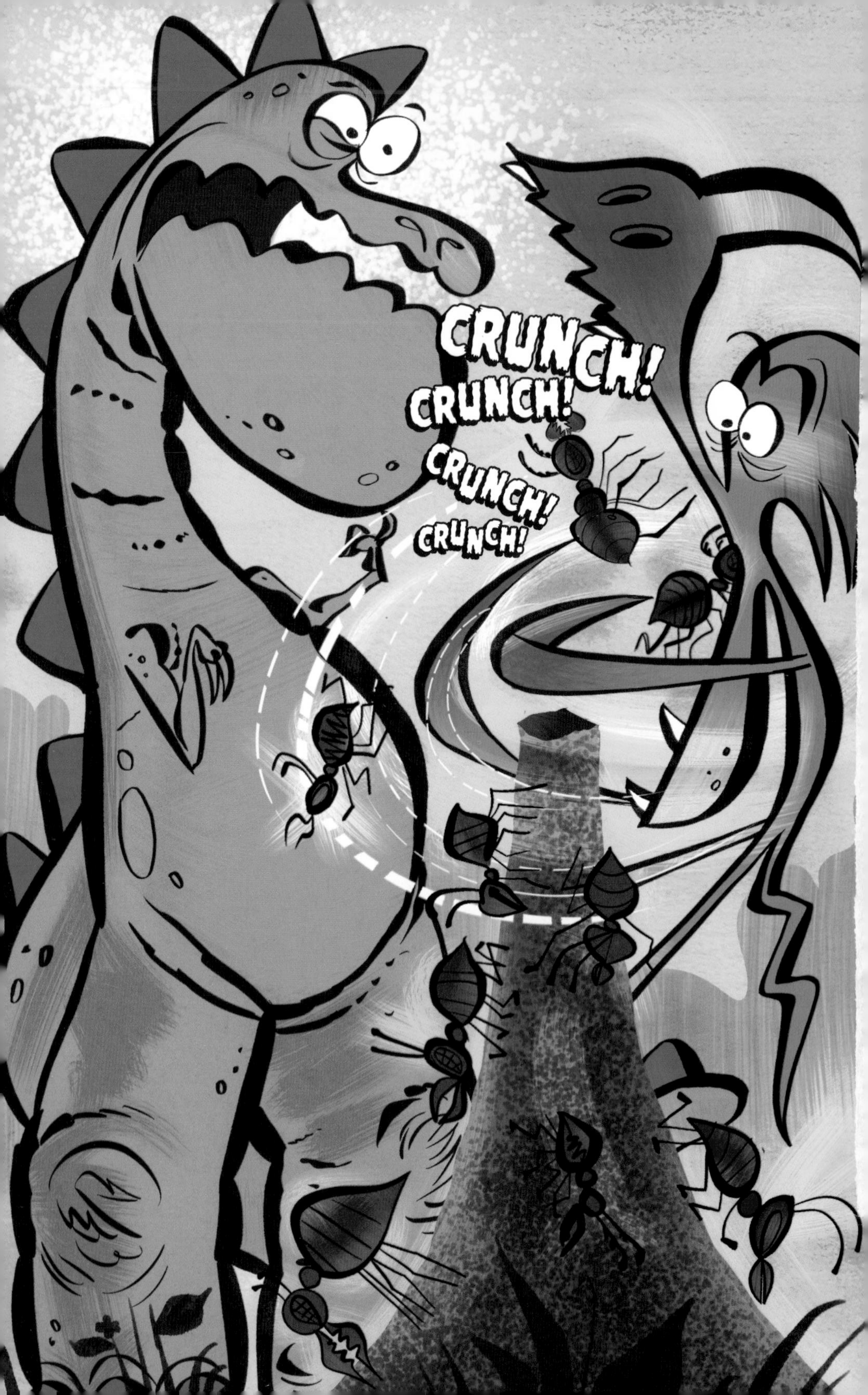
CRUNCH!
CRUNCH!
CRUNCH!
CRUNCH!

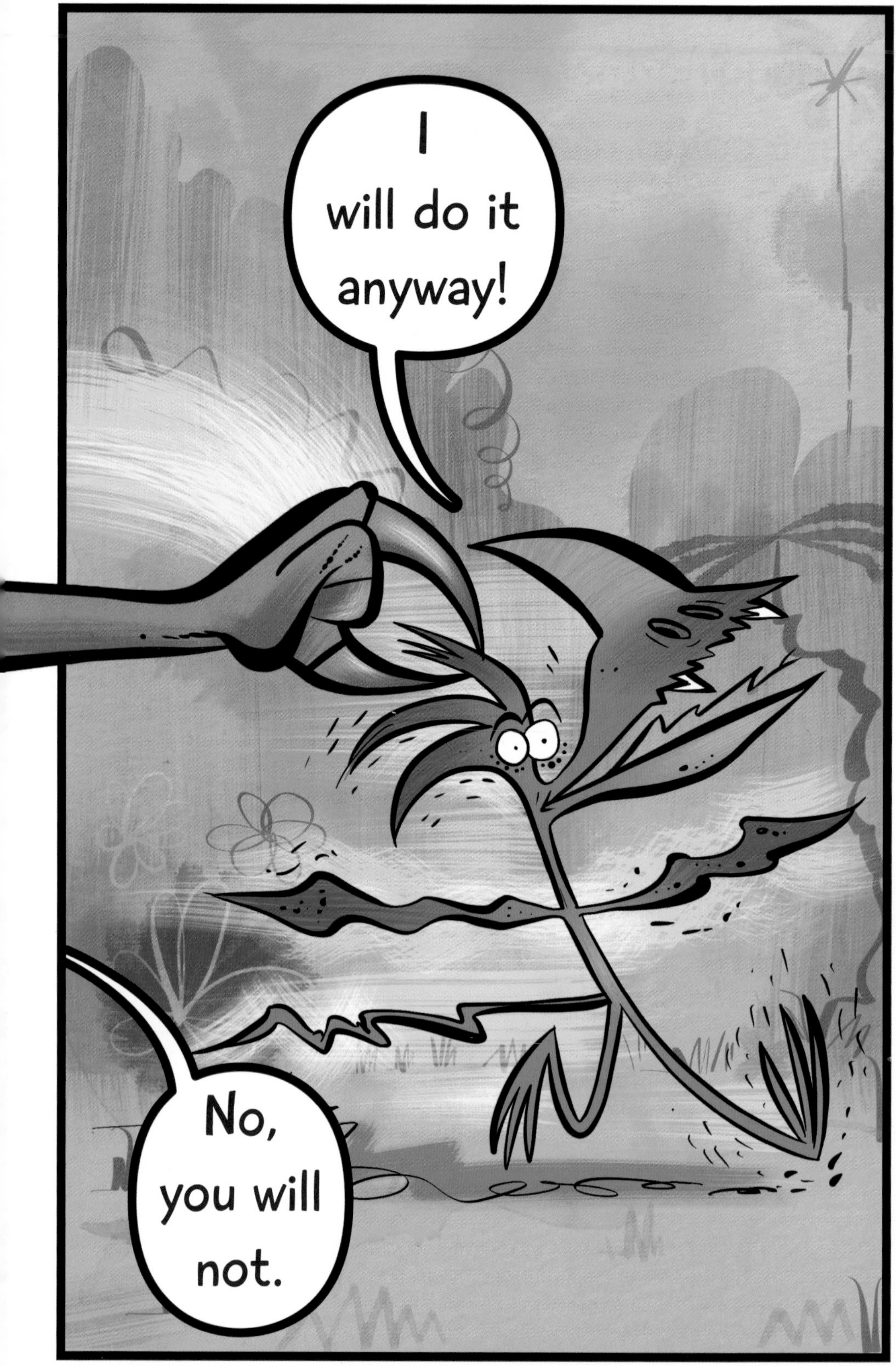
I will do it anyway!
No, you will not.

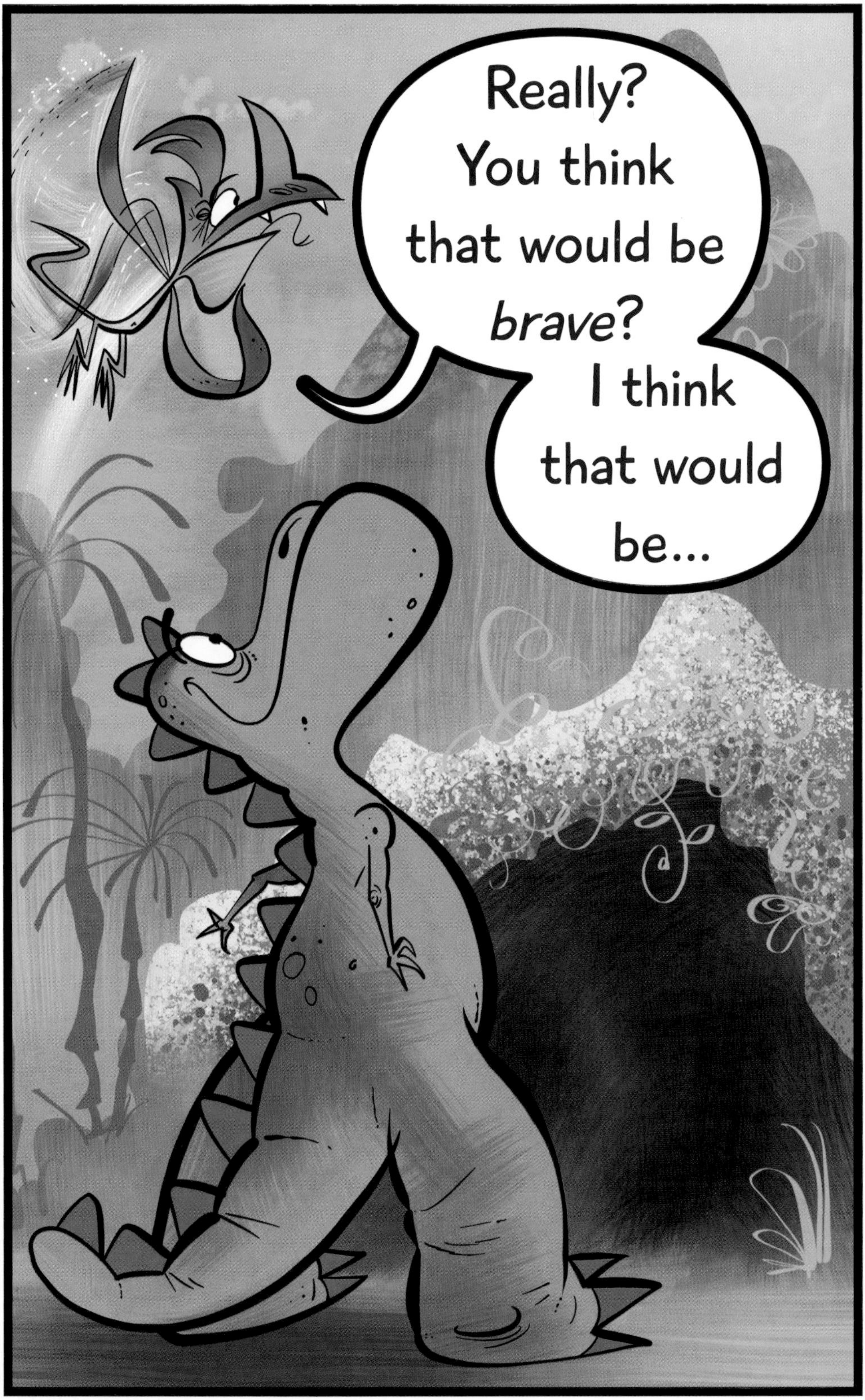
Really? You think that would be *brave*?
I think that would be...

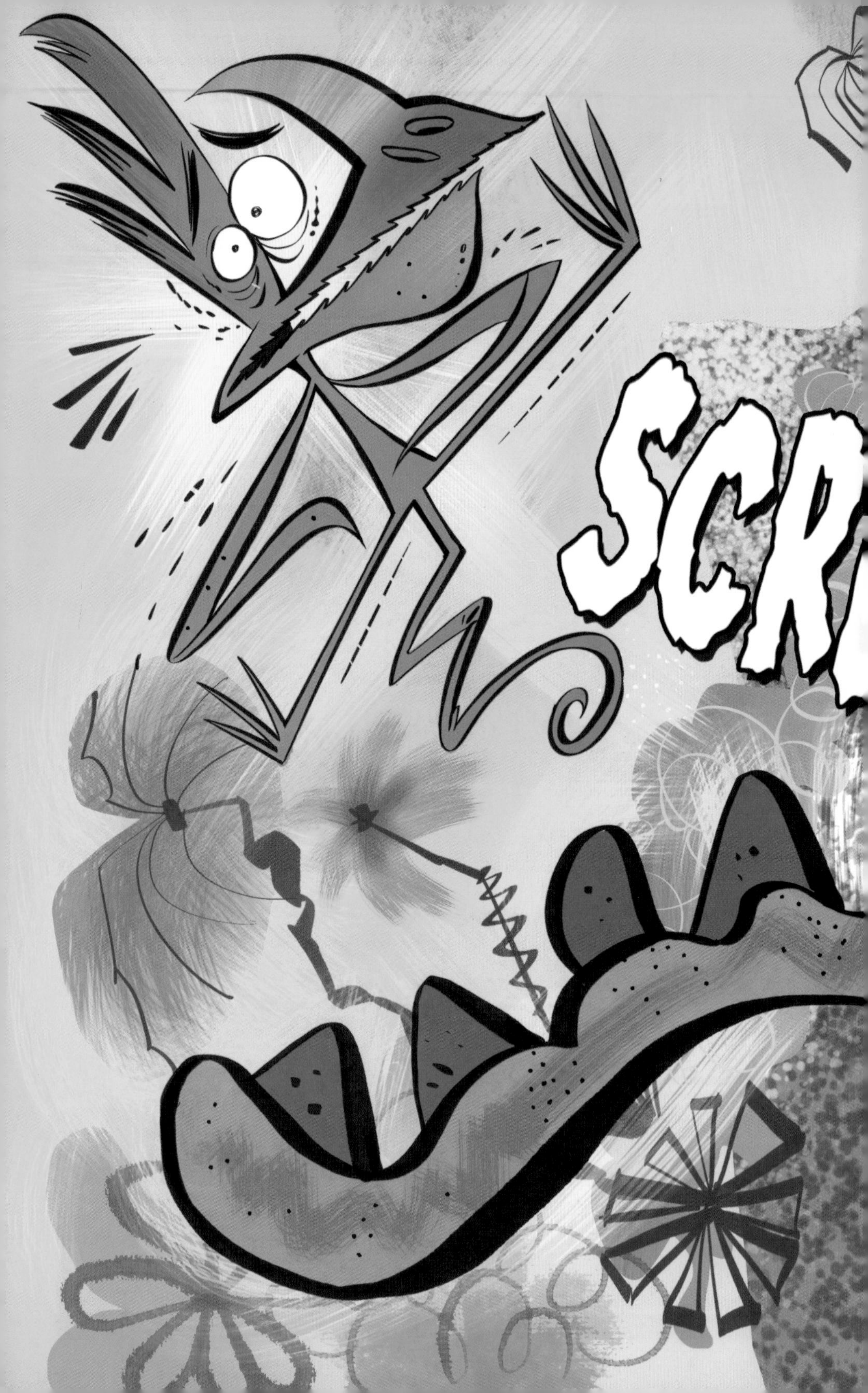
SCR

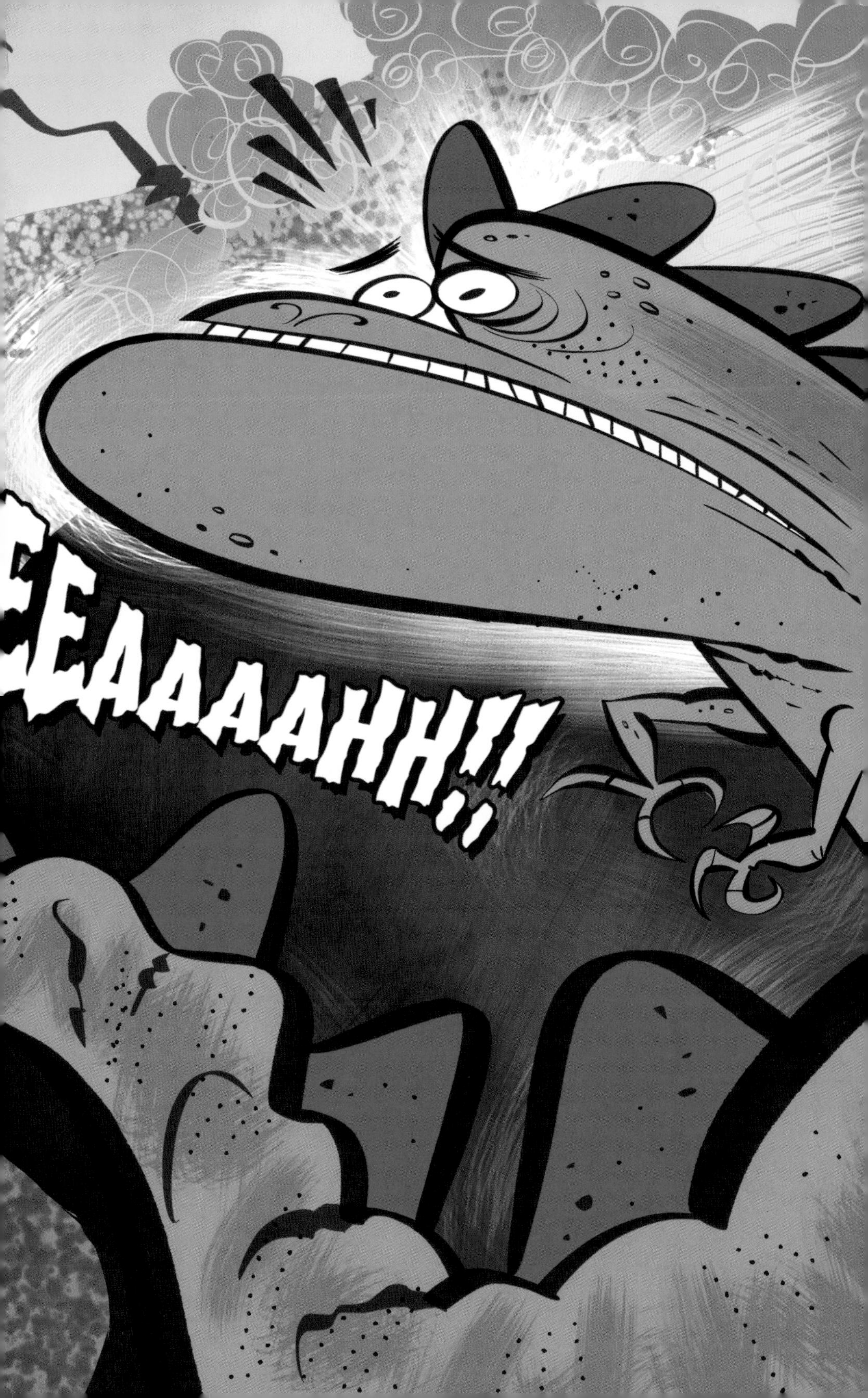
EEAAAAAHH!!

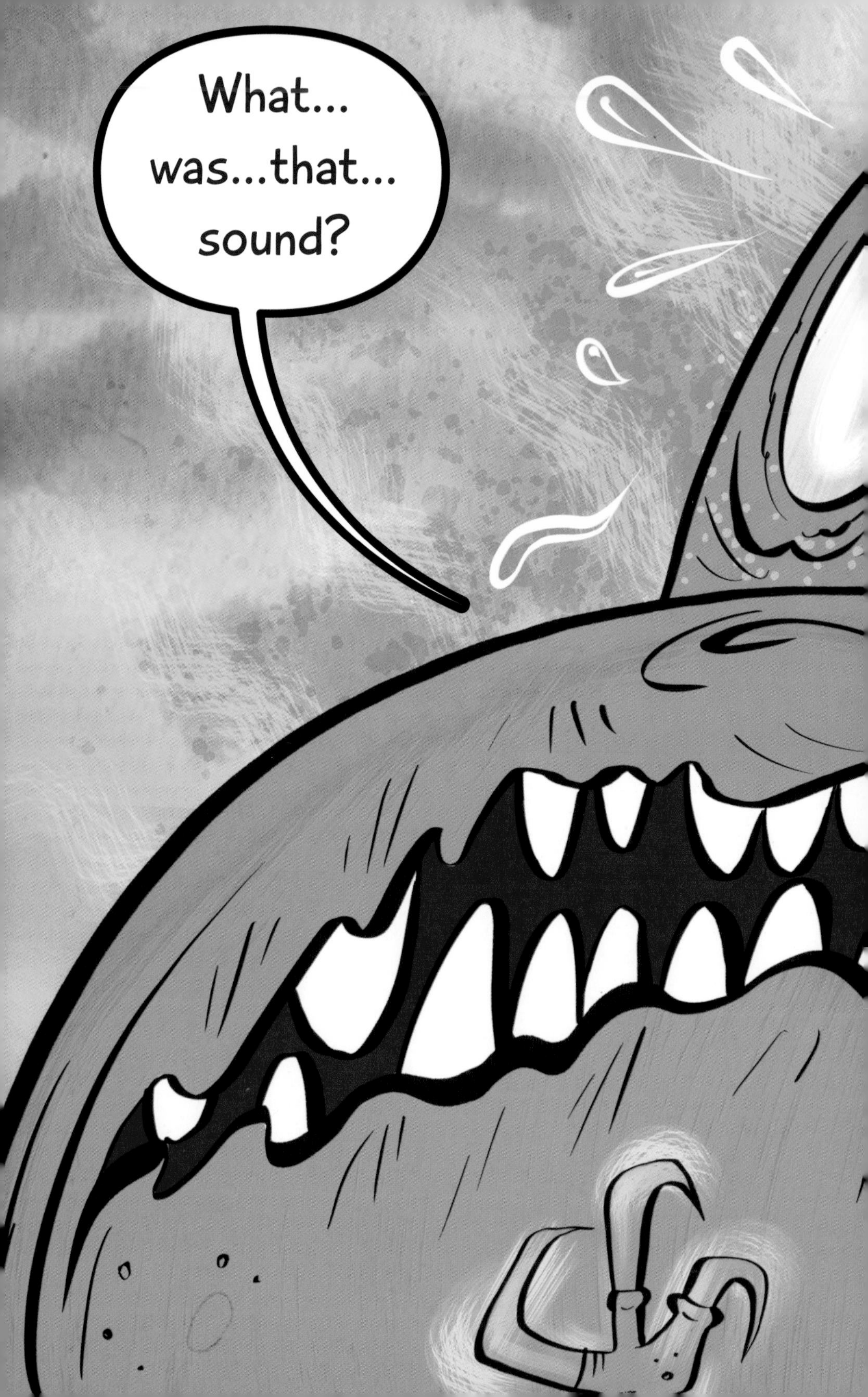
What... was...that... sound?

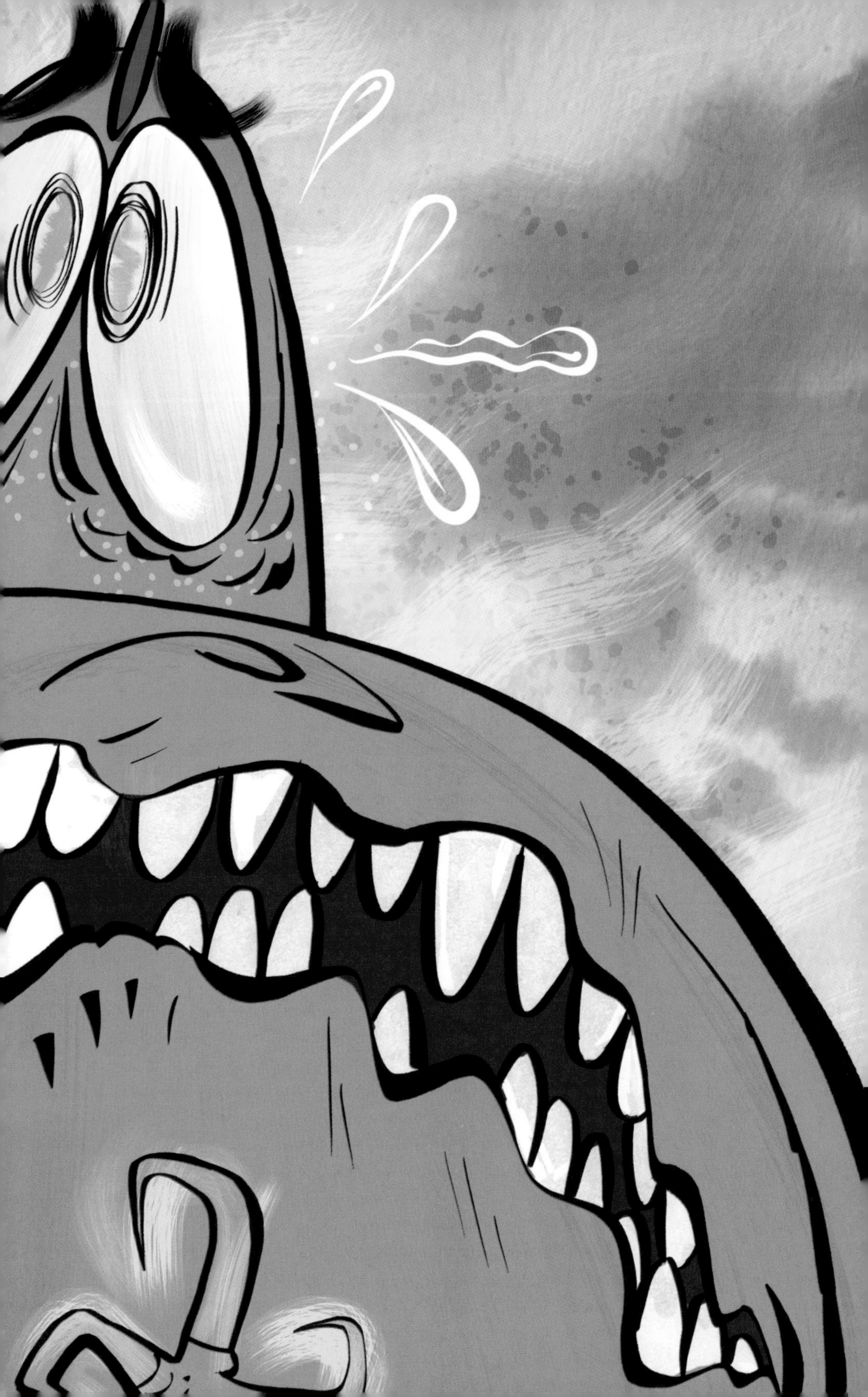

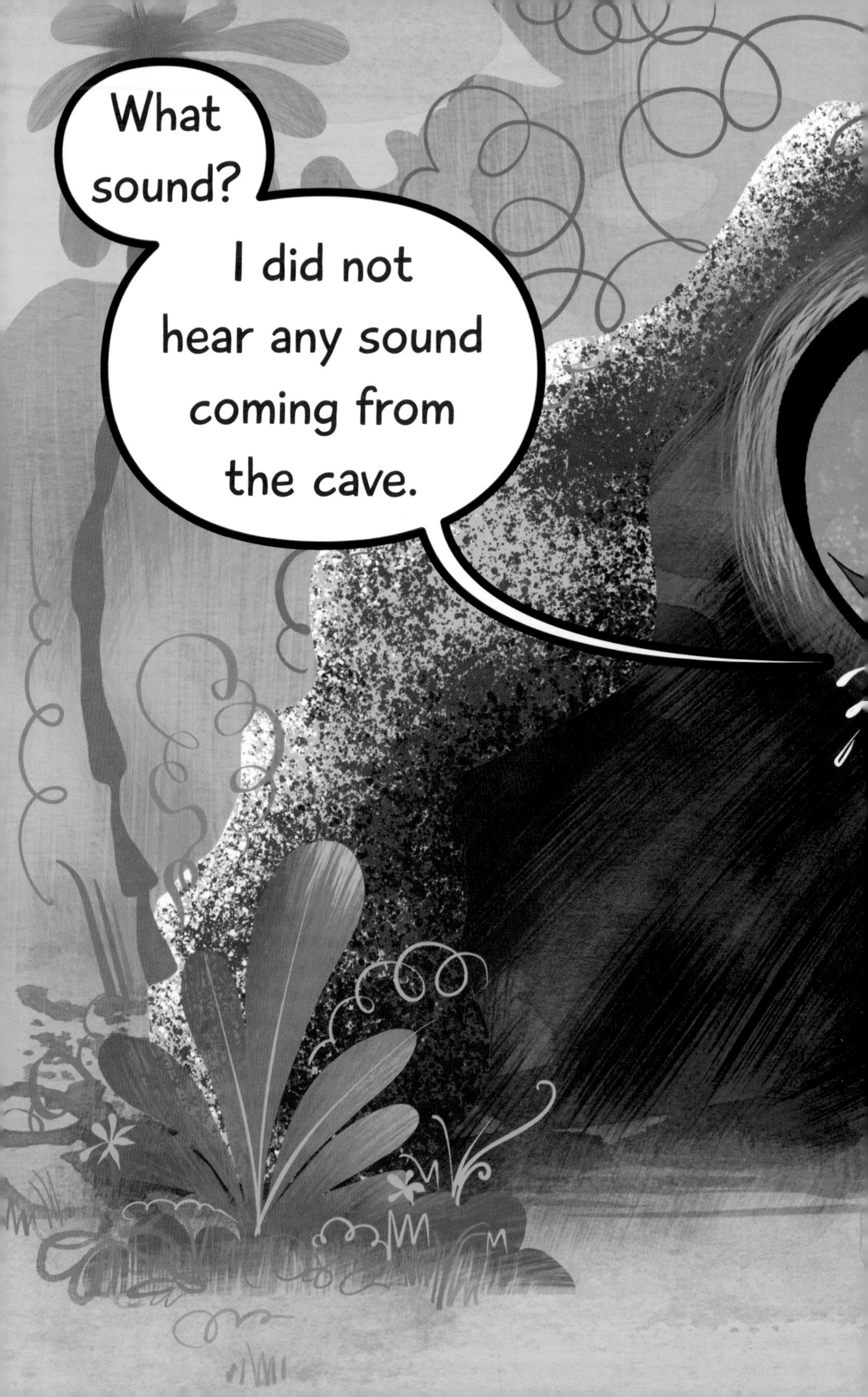
What sound?
I did not hear any sound coming from the cave.

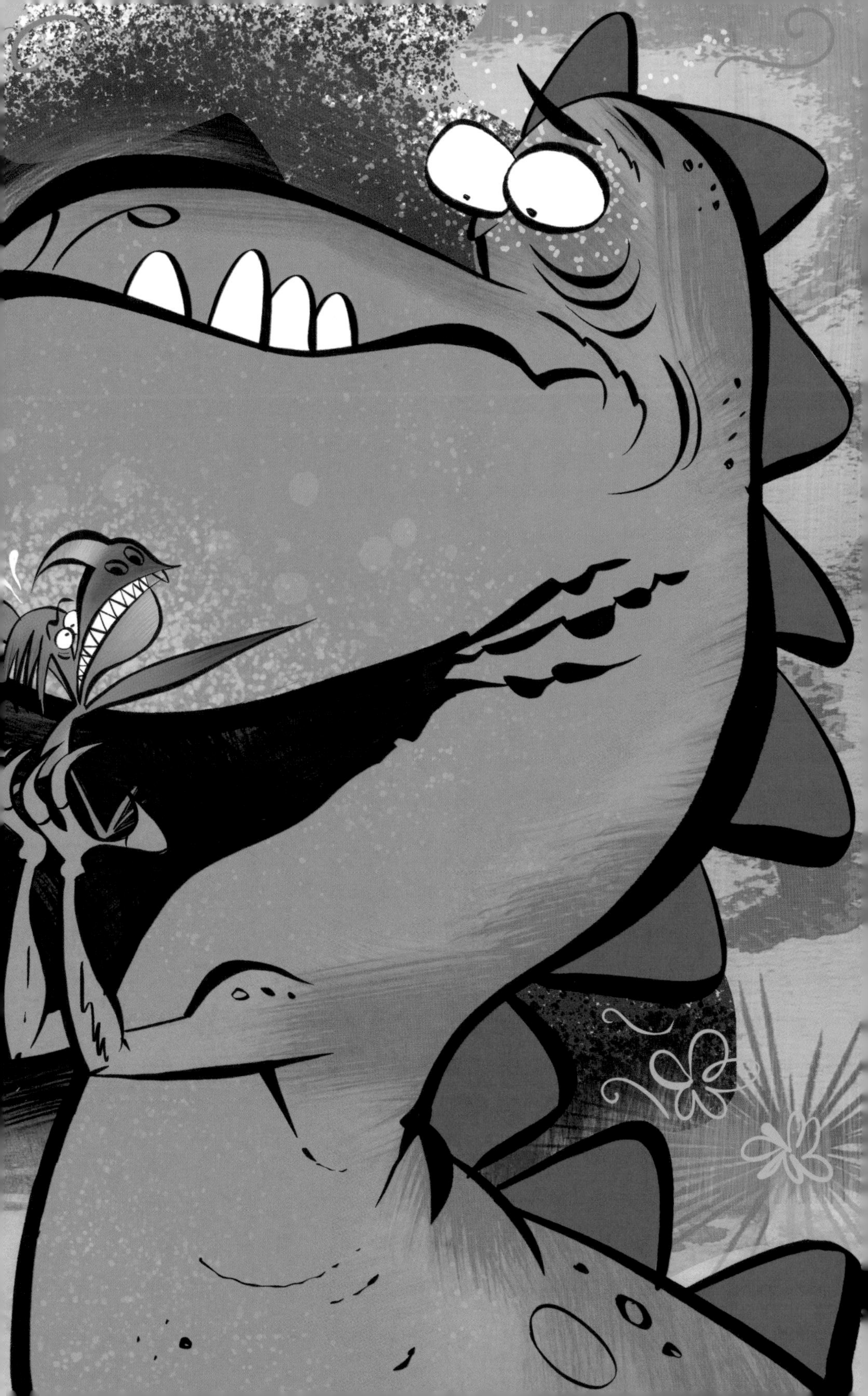

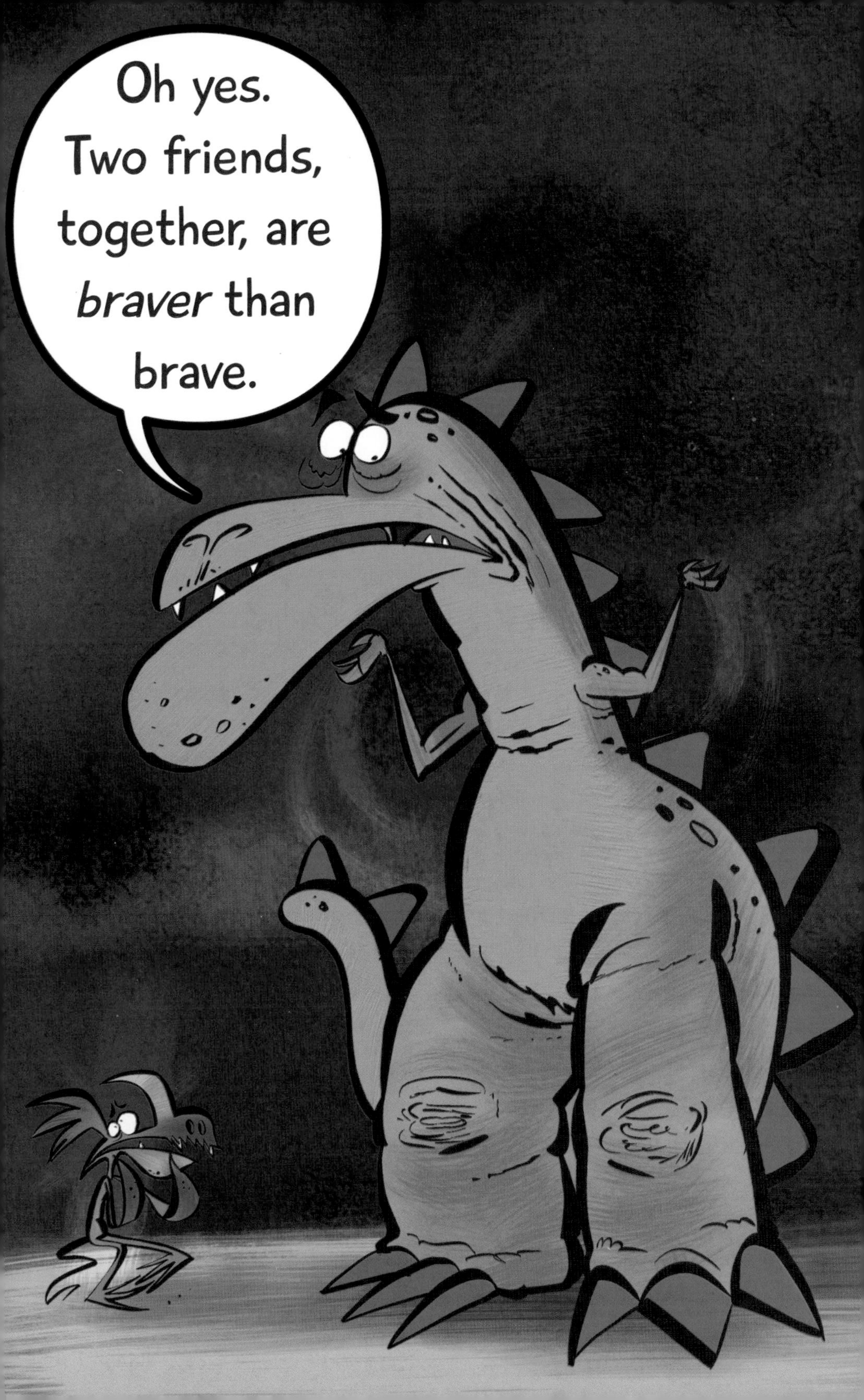
Oh yes. Two friends, together, are *braver* than brave.

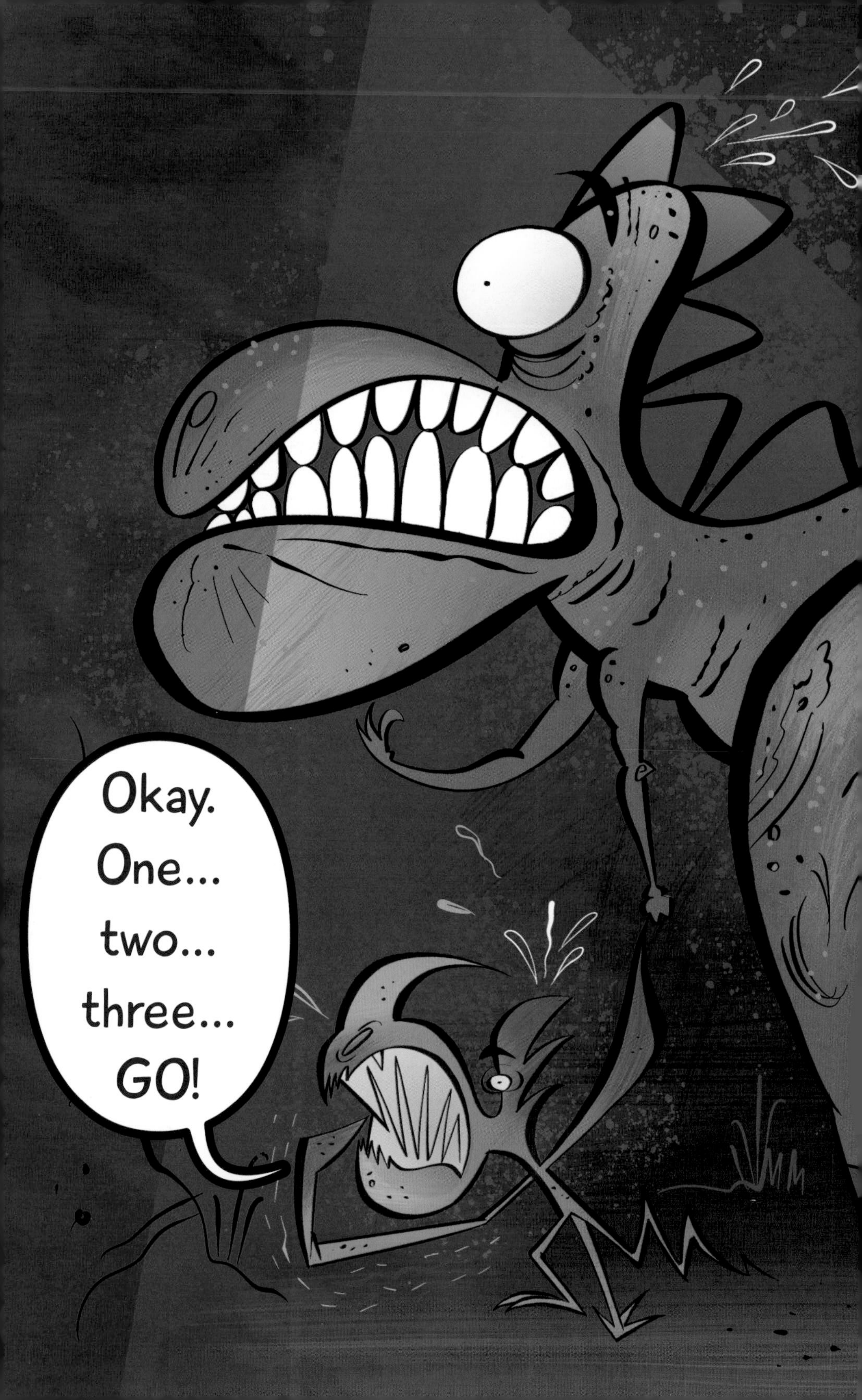
Okay. One... two... three... GO!

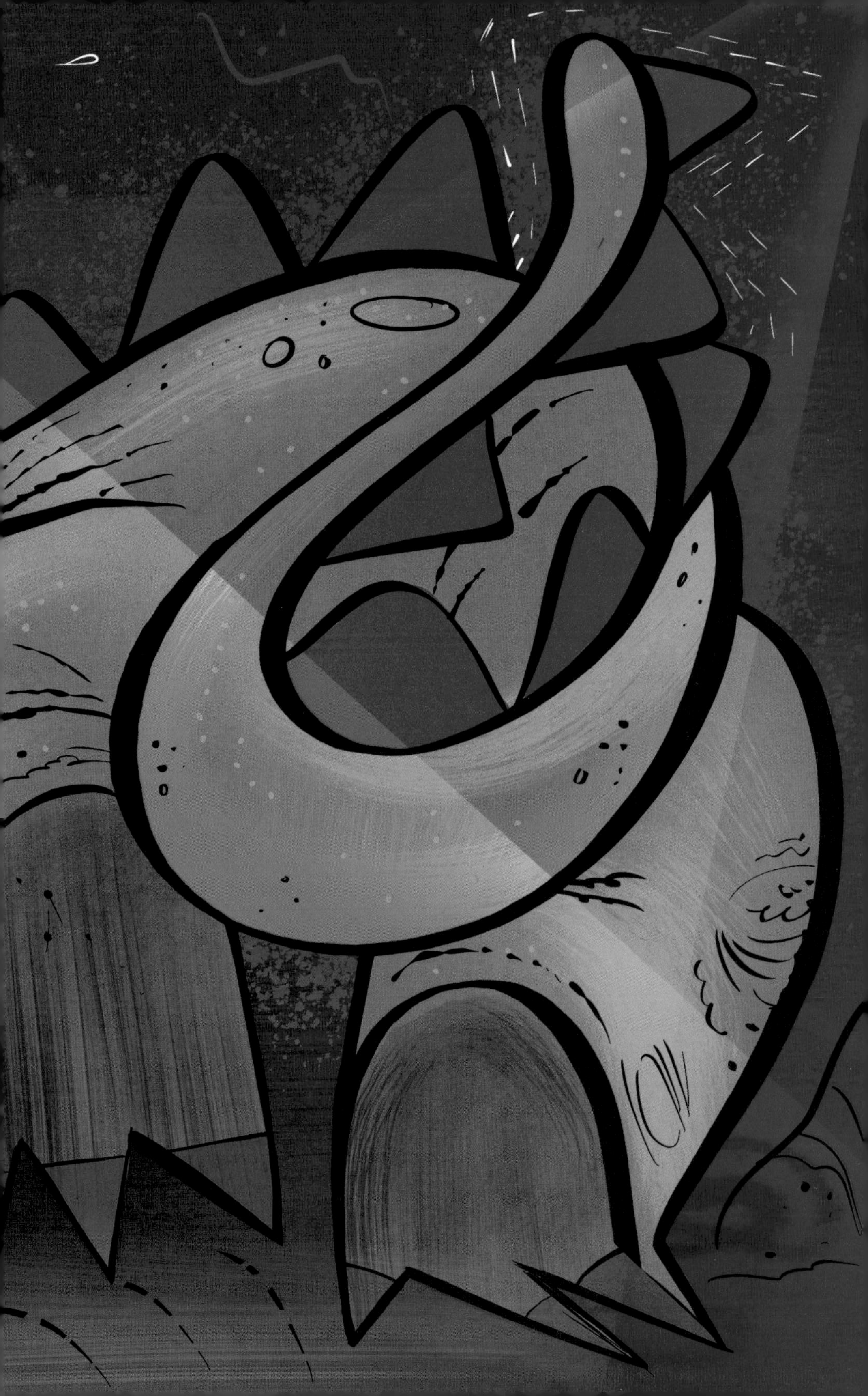

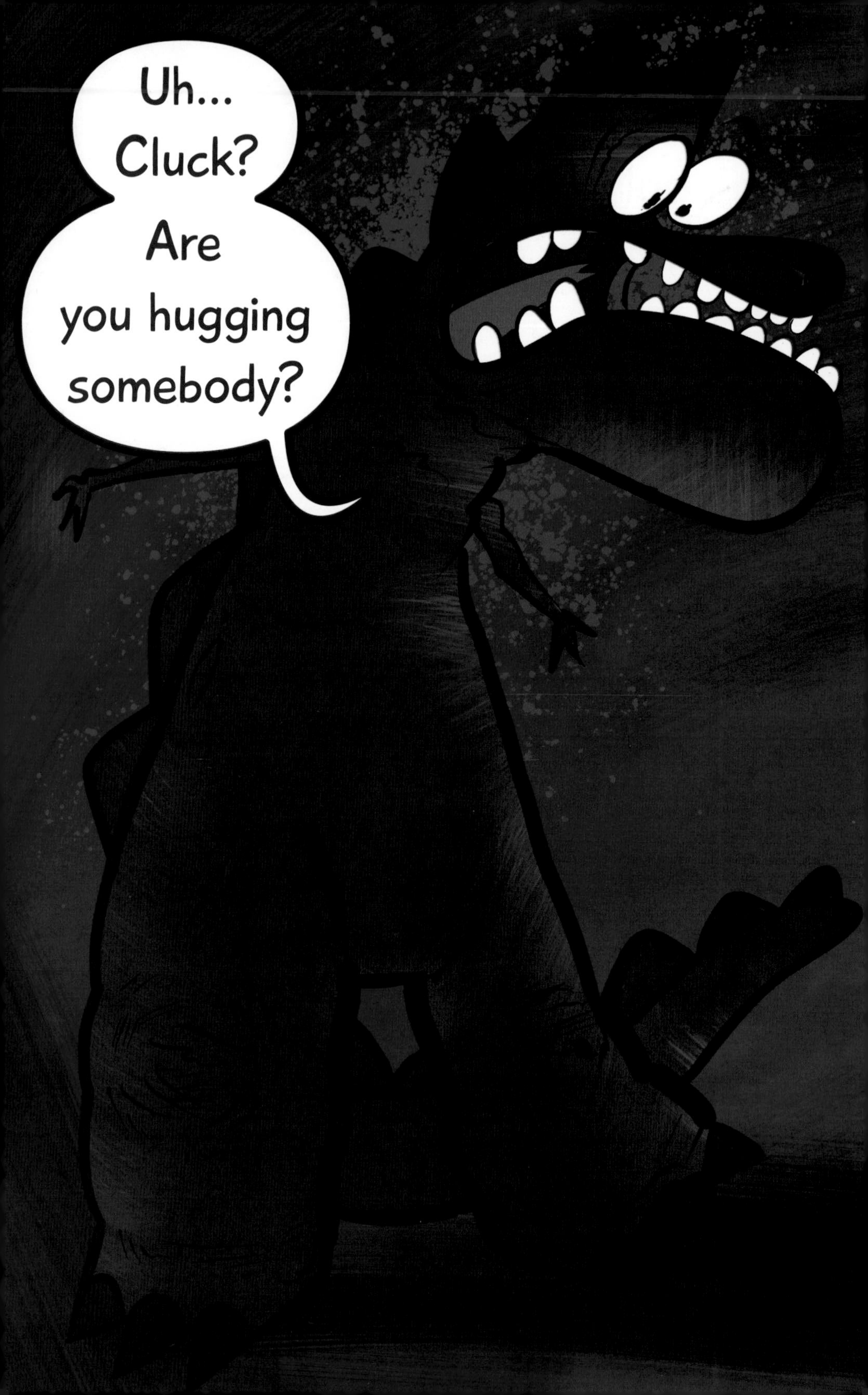
Uh... Cluck? Are you hugging somebody?

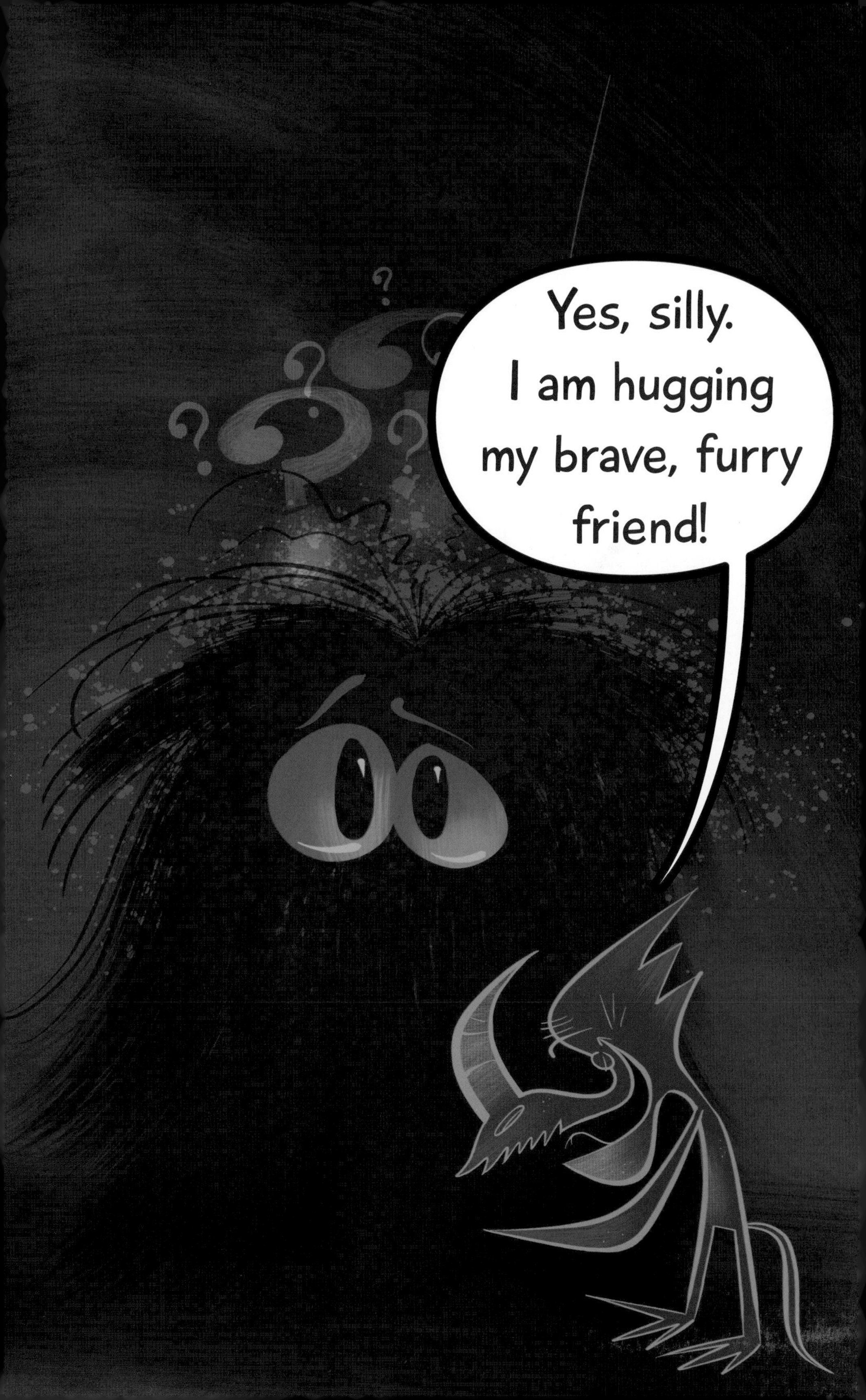
Yes, silly. I am hugging my brave, furry friend!

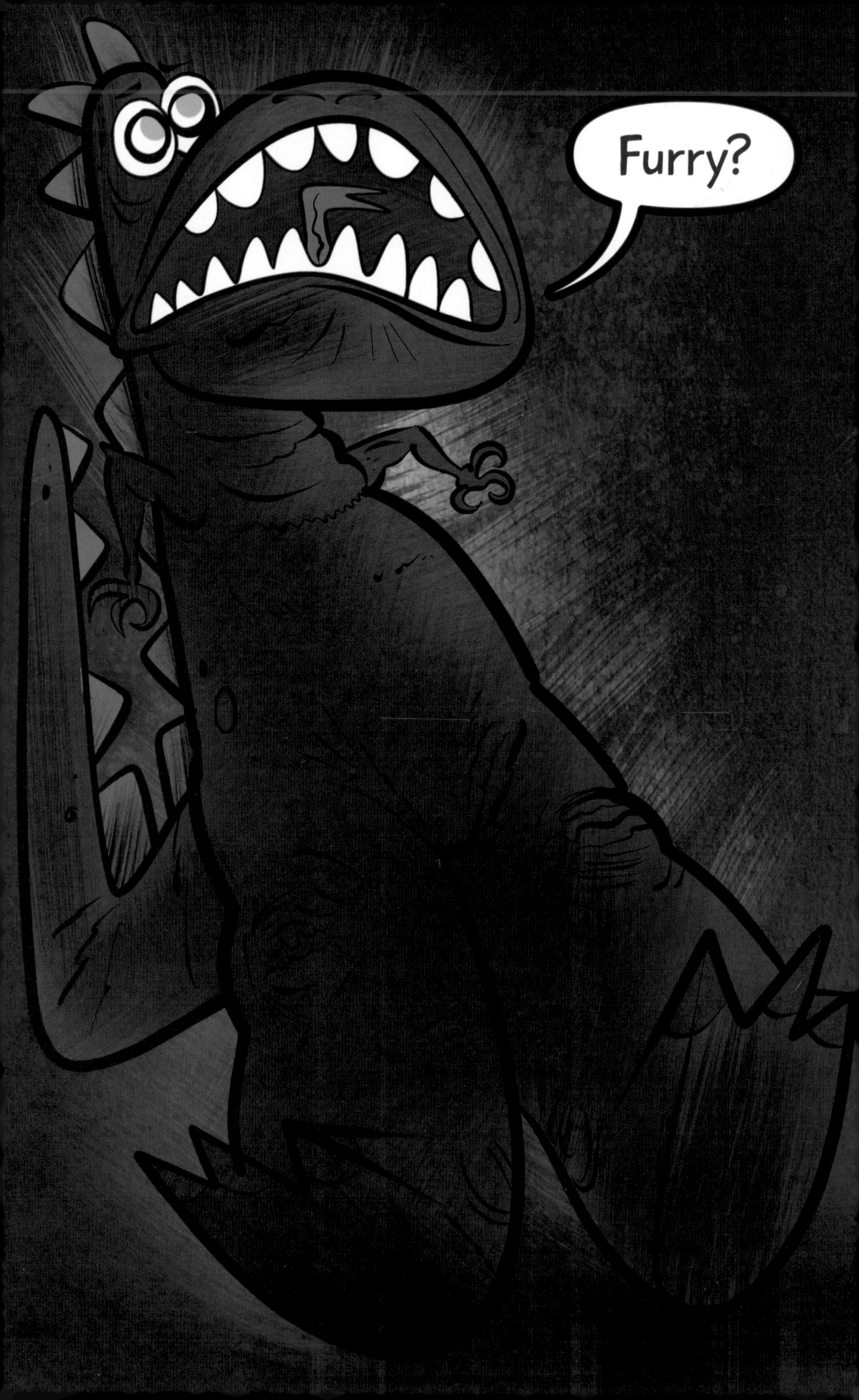
Furry?

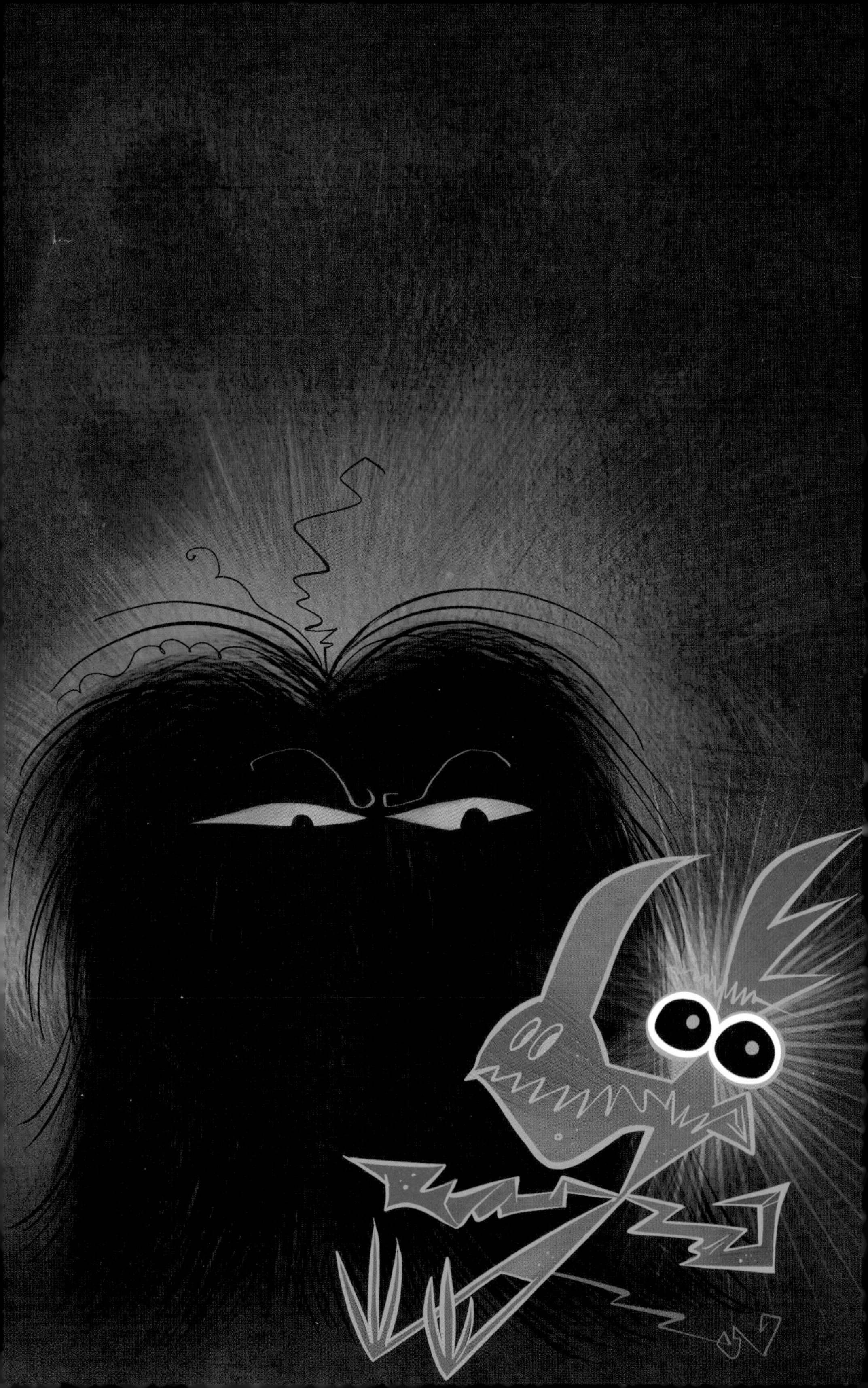

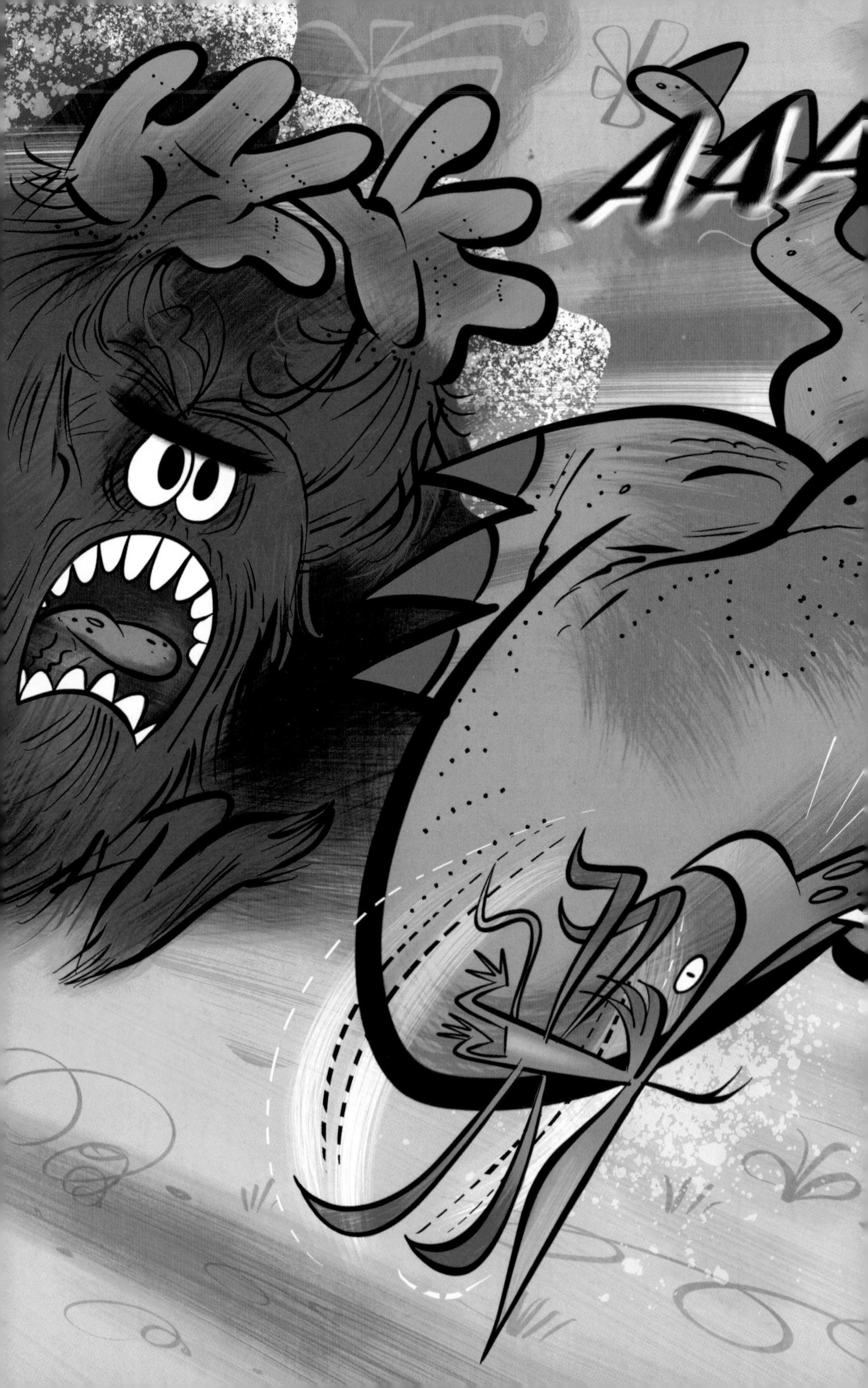
AAA

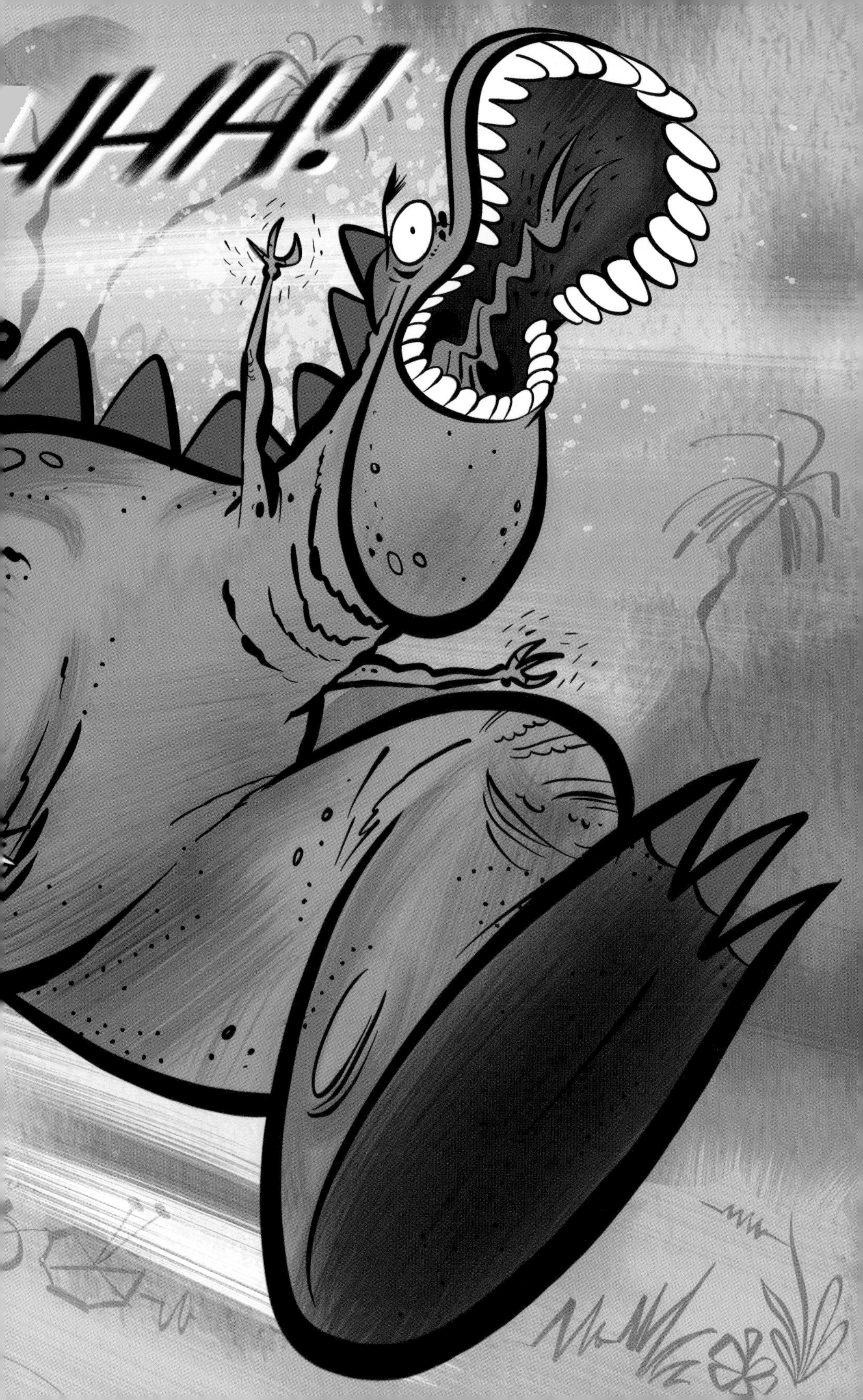
HH!

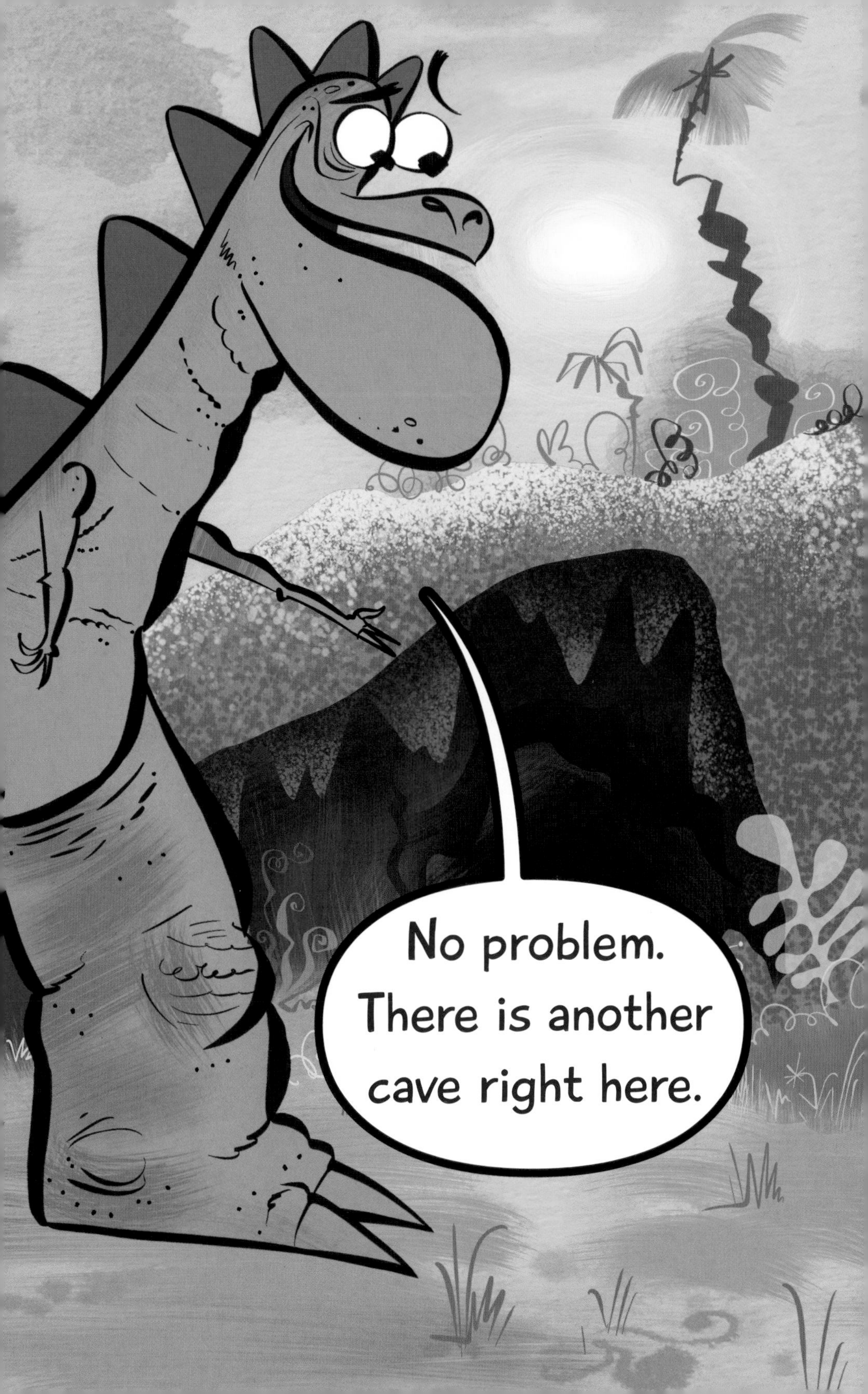
No problem. There is another cave right here.

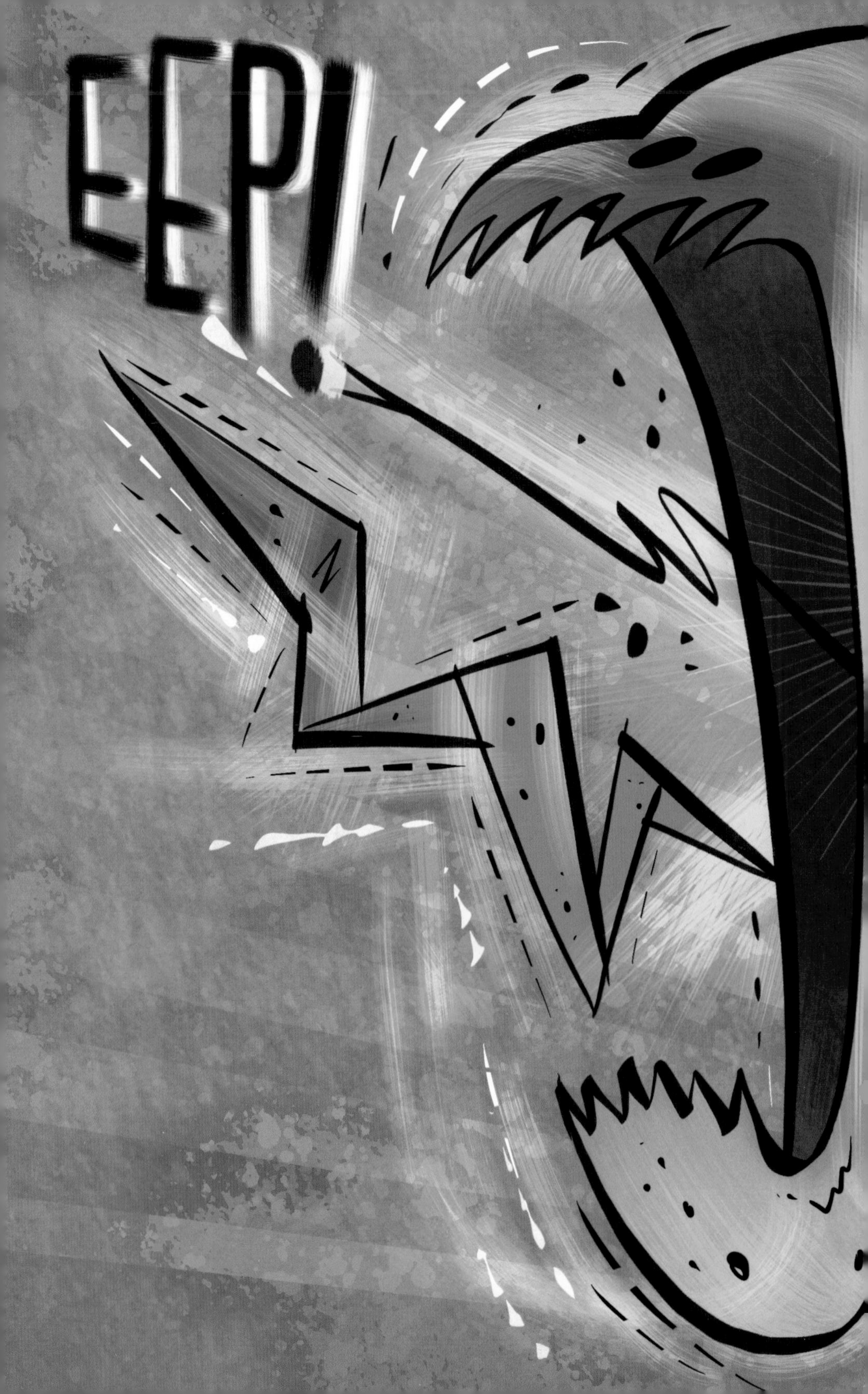
EEP!